Animal Instinct

It was the perfect hold-up, conducted with military precision by four men who calmly walked out of the Ozark Branch of the First National Bank with close to $50,000.

Then it all went wrong.

One unfortunate shot hits their leader Frank Jerome as he rides away. What to do? Take the risk and try to ride out the 250 miles back to the mighty Mississippi? Or let the other three escape without being slowed by a wounded man?

Frank didn't hesitate. In a selfless act he stayed to face a prison sentence and an uncertain future. Now, years later on release, his companions have all disappeared along with the money, and it is going to take more than luck to untangle the lies, deceit and secrets that have been left behind. It is going to take animal instinct.

Animal Instinct

Lee Clinton

A Black Horse Western

ROBERT HALE

ISBN 978-0-7198-3146-1

The Crowood Press
The Stable Block
Crowood Lane
Ramsbury
Marlborough
Wiltshire SN8 2HR

www.bhwesterns.com

Robert Hale is an imprint
of The Crowood Press

For QT
This is my number 10

Typeset by
Simon and Sons ITES Services Pvt Ltd
Printed and bound in Great Britain by
4Bind Ltd, Stevenage, SG1 2XT

ONE

1875: RED LEFT HAND

Ozark, Missouri

Just when he thought they were clear, Frank got shot. Up till then the hold-up had gone off like clockwork.

The four had ridden up to the front of the Ozark Branch of the First National on Hall Street, right at that quiet time around mid-afternoon. Three dismounted as one, leaving Bic on lookout with the horses. Frank, Coops and Ray stepped up on to the boardwalk, and at a sharp pace entered the front door in single file. Ray immediately turned to the right and stopped, hand on gun, to stand guard. John Cooper peeled off from behind Frank to take up a position on the side wall to the left, in the centre, near the bench used for filling out deposit and withdrawal forms. Coops' right hand was also on his gun, in his left was a small silver pocket watch, which he glanced at and announced in a strong clear voice, 'Look this way. This won't take long and you will not be harmed provided you remain perfectly still and put your hands on your head. Do not make me repeat myself.'

The four customers standing in line, three men and an elderly woman, all obliged without a murmur. Cooper thanked them for their assistance.

Frank, who held a well-worn US Cavalry saddlebag in his left hand, was now at the front counter and addressed the lone teller, Mr Martin Buckley. 'Hands where I can see them. Move to the door and let me in.'

No guns had been drawn and indeed none would be removed from their holsters throughout the duration of the robbery, which would last for no longer than two and half minutes. The manner in which these men conducted their illegal business was with a clear sense of purpose and precision, as often displayed with authority on a military parade ground.

The teller did precisely as he was told and let Frank in, before being directed to open the six-foot-tall safe manufactured by the Barnes Safe & Lock Company of Pittsburgh. The doors were closed but unlocked.

'One minute,' came the call from Coops.

They were precisely on time as Frank put his hand on the first of the nine neatly bound bundles on the bottom shelf. Each contained currency of $5,000 in various denominations of five, ten and twenty-dollar bills and weighed approximately two pounds. The tenth bundle had been broken open. Frank assessed the amount removed, when placing this last packet in the left side compartment of the saddlebag, to be around fifteen hundred dollars short. He buckled the straps on both flaps while still kneeling in front of the safe, stood, nodded to the teller who opened the counter door for him to leave.

Coops called two minutes.

Frank walked straight to the front door and stopped beside Ray and handed him the saddlebag, which now weighed approximately twenty pounds. Coops walked past both Frank and Ray to join Bic and the horses. Ray followed while Frank remained on guard just inside the door. The bag was handed to Bic who positioned it to the front of his saddle, while Coops and Ray mounted.

'OK,' came the call from Coops. Frank responded with 'OK', and walked briskly across the boardwalk, took the reins from Bic and said, 'Go!'. All three took off as Frank mounted. He looked around to check that it was clear before flicking the end of the reins right and left while kicking back his heels. His fine horse of sixteen hands leapt forwards and in twenty yards was close to a full gallop. The other three riders were nearing the end of the street when a single rifle shot cracked the air.

The wallop of the high-speed .44 Winchester round as it hit into Frank's upper left leg was instantly followed by white-hot pain from his waist to his ankle. His immediate reflex was to drop his left hand and grasp at the wound. He felt the flow of wet, warm blood, causing him to look down. The fabric to the knee was already dark red. 'Geezus!' he cried out through clenched teeth as he pulled back on the reins and drew his Navy revolver. His horse skidded and reared as it came to a halt, with Frank searching for the whereabouts of his assailant – yet all look quiet, except for a slight movement a little way back up the street on the other side, at the end of a water trough. It was a boot – a small brown boot. 'Geezus,' repeated Frank. 'Come on kid, stand up and show yourself.'

'You'll shoot me,' came the juvenile voice from behind the trough.

'If I'd wanted to shoot you, I'd've done it already, now stand up.'

Sheepishly the youth stood, the warm Winchester in his hand, barrel down.

'What the hell were you thinking of, discharging a firearm in a main street? You could have killed somebody, a neighbour, some innocent, even a woman. You could have shot this horse if you hadn't found my leg first. Talk about all the dumb things to do. How old are you?'

'Twelve. Thirteen next week.'

'If you were ten, you'd still be old enough to know better.'

'You're bleeding real bad,' came the observation.

'You bet I am. You got me in the leg, and I'm going to need plugging pretty fast!'

A high-pitched whistle shrilled. It was Coops trying to get Frank's attention as the three remained stationary at the end of the street. Frank responded by holding up his red left hand, then waved for them to go. The three turned their horses back towards Frank. He shook his head and gave another vigorous wave for them to go. He had to do it a third time before they took off, but not before John Cooper, James Bicknell and Ray Nelson all saluted in farewell.

Frank turned to the kid who remained perfectly still behind the water trough. 'What's your name?'

'Len.'

'Len what?'

'Len, sir.'

'No, your surname?'

'Len Aspin.'

'Len Aspin, which way to the doctor's?'

'Back up past the bank to the top of the hill, then turn right. White house third down. The one before the old oak.'

'What's the Doc's name?'

'Doc Milburn.'

'And the sheriff. What's his name?'

'Sheriff Kalie.'

'Will you please give my compliments to Sheriff Kalie and ask if he could meet me at Doc's place?'

'Now, sir?'

'Yes, now.'

Len turned then stopped. 'Are you going to tell my parents?'

'No, I'll leave you to do that.'

'They won't be none too pleased with what I done. Shooting at an adult.'

'Nor me, but what's done is done.' Frank grimaced as he turned his horse back up the street and began to canter towards the top of the hill.

'Sorry, mister,' shouted young Len.

Frank gave a wave but didn't look back as he said under his breath, 'And me.'

TWO

LOYAL BOYS

Doc Milburn's

'Doc, you in there?' came the yell.

'Out the back,' came the reply.

'Are you OK?'

'I'm fine, come on through.'

'You sure?'

'Sure, I'm sure.'

The sheriff seemed to take forever before he eventually poked his nose around the corner to where Doc Milburn treated his patients. His handgun was drawn.

'Afternoon sheriff,' said Frank.

'And who are you?'

'Frank Jerome.'

'Are you on your own?'

'I am.'

'Where are the others?'

11

'Gone.'

'Gone where?'

'Can't say. Our plan was for each to go their own separate way, to make it harder for you to follow.'

'How many of you were there?'

'Four, including me.' Frank knew the game, tell the sheriff what he already knows or would find out from the witnesses.

'You can put your gun away sheriff,' said the Doc. 'Frank here isn't going anywhere. He's lost a bit of blood and is going to lose a bit more before I get the bullet out. It's still in the leg, somewhere.' The doctor was getting ready to insert a probe to find out exactly where.

'He's still armed,' said the sheriff.

'Then take his gun.' The Doc was busy and getting a little irritated.

'I'll give it to you if you want,' said Frank.

'No, don't you move.' The sheriff edged over slowly, pistol still drawn, as he reached out and gently slipped the Navy Colt from the holster while keeping his eyes on Frank.

'You can put that away now, Tom,' advised the doctor.

Sheriff Kalie holstered his gun, albeit a little reluctantly. 'Most men would have ridden off, taken their chance,' said the sheriff.

'I'm not most men,' said Frank.

'Why is that?'

'You could call it instinct, or maybe it has more to do with being shot once before. I kind of know what follows.'

'Shot where?'

'In the shoulder.'

'Robbing another bank?'

'Nope, at Champion Hill.'

'Champion Hill,' repeated the sheriff. 'When was that?'

'May 16,'62.'

'Who were you with?'

'Company B, 3rd Missouri Cavalry, but we were dismounted for that battle. In fact, most battles. We were a poor man's cavalry unit. They rarely gave us a ride. Seemed to walk everywhere.'

'Green's brigade?'

'That's the one.'

'Damn it,' cussed the sheriff. 'What do you loyal boys think you are doing, going bushwhacking?'

'You know Green's brigade, then?'

'Of course I do. I served in Bowen's division.'

'Small world,' said Frank with a grimace.

'Found it.' The doc withdrew the thin steel probe. 'Best I take that bullet out now.'

'Your call,' said Frank.

'Even after all that time fighting and living hard, you still weren't tempted to make a run for it?' asked the sheriff.

'Nope, I would only have slowed down the others, and the wound needed plugging. I reckon I would have fallen off my horse by about now. And then there's the infection. I've seen men lose a limb from blood poisoning.' Frank added, 'If they managed to stay alive, that is.'

The sheriff wasn't going to argue, he'd seen the same. 'You're not from around these parts, are you?'

Frank just shook his head as he held his breath. The doctor now began to insert the long needle-nosed forceps.

'The other three?'

Frank shook his head again.

'And you're not going to tell me where they are from, are you?'

Another shake of the head.

'And I'm guessing they are loyal boys also.'

Frank remained silent.

'I thought so. Damn it.'

'Got it,' said the doc. 'Just need to ease it out, slowly, don't move a muscle.'

Frank was sweating blood, but he didn't move a hair on his head.

The sheriff moved closer. 'Here, grab my hand.'

Frank's grip was like a vice. Or it was, right up to the time he passed out.

'Sweet dreams,' observed the doc.

The sheriff still held Frank's hand. 'We're going to see more of this, mark my words.'

'More of what?' The doc was just about there.

'Loyal boys going rogue.'

'Come on, come on, just about there.' The doc was coaxing the lead round out of the puncture wound to the thigh muscle.

'And you know what?' said the sheriff, 'I don't blame them. Who can? 3rd Cavalry was tough as buffalo hide, but what did they get to show for their loyalty? No jobs, no opportunity, no future, just damn reconstruction and carpetbaggers. No wonder these boys are going rogue.'

THREE

1864: THE BATTLE OF WESTPORT

Eleven Years Before – 23 October 1864

'We need a volunteer.'

All stood in line, eyes downcast, concentrating, as if to find an answer from their muddy boots to an unfathomable question.

'It's a good job,' said the sergeant with a smile, or maybe it was a smirk. Hard to tell in the fading light. Anyway, nobody was falling for the smooth, persuasive Southern talk. They'd been caught before.

Frank lifted his head just a fraction to see what was going on. It was a bad move. The sergeant was looking directly at him. He promptly dropped his head, but it was too late.

'Good, we have our volunteer.'

The shoulders of the others fell in relief.

Frank whispered under his breath, 'Geezus, why did I do that?'

'It's a great job, Frank. Dispatch riding. Perfect for a wounded veteran.'

'I'm not wounded, my shoulder's fine.'

'I know it is. If you hadn't volunteered, I would have chosen you anyway.'

Frank was going to say, then why did we just go through all that … He cut short his thoughts and half smiled, it made for a good joke. Trouble was, the joke was on him.

'You're being attached to Uncle Joe's headquarters, and knowing you to be a fine soldier, I'm sure you will represent the 3rd Cavalry in all its glory. And this time you will be mounted and not on foot, as we horsemen have mostly been for the best part of this war. So, what do you say?'

'Yes, sergeant. Thank you, sergeant.'

'Good man. However, you will still have to walk over to the brigade headquarters to get your horse.'

'How far?' asked Frank.

'Next door. Only a mile.'

Someone from the ranks quipped, 'Ride 'em cowboy,' and the others laughed.

'Squad.' All stiffened to the sergeant's order. 'Dismiss.'

As the men shuffled away, the sergeant walked forward to Frank and placed his hand lightly on his shoulder. 'You'll be on your own. Just keep using that good head of yours and you'll be OK. The others weren't up to it. Not yet. Not like you.'

Frank nodded in appreciation of the compliment, and he felt his chest expand a little with pride. 'I'll do my best.'

'I'm sure you will. You have enough time to grab some chow before you kit up. Just be back here in thirty. The company orderly room will provide you with your pass, pistol, belt and holster before you leave for General Shelby's HQ.'

'I don't need to eat. I'd prefer to leave now. If it's all the same.'

'OK,' said the sergeant. 'I understand.'

* * *

The major from Shelby's HQ handed Frank the leather wallet. 'Tuck this inside your jacket. It contains the field orders for Colonel Jackman. In the event of imminent capture, bury the dispatches and get as far away as you can. If you're caught, tell the Federals that you had got lost when trying to return to the rear to escort troops forwards.'

Who's going to believe that? thought Frank. He'd never known of a lone rider escorting troops forwards. Guides came in pairs and were never mounted, they marched everywhere on foot, like everybody else in the 3rd Cavalry.

'Do you understand?' said the major.

'Yes, sir. Riding to the rear to escort troops forward.'

'Good. Now these are your directions – commit them to memory. Follow the creek down for a mile and a half, where you will see a ford just beyond the remains of the old wooden bridge. Cross at that point.' The major was pointing to the map on the small folding table before them. 'Continue north for a further two miles and you will meet up with our right flank. The challenge will be "silver", your response is "sabre". Identify yourself as an Iron Brigade dispatch rider and you will be escorted to Colonel Jackman's headquarters. Any questions?'

'No, sir.' Sounds simple enough, thought Frank.

'Good luck.'

Frank saluted. 'Thank you, sir.'

* * *

Frank was just about to cross the ford near the remains of the old wooden bridge when he was challenged. He stopped and waited for the word 'silver', when he realized that he was facing a group of Federals. Instinctively he turned and bolted his horse to a full gallop down a lane beside the river as a volley of shots passed over his head. He'd been told the Iron Brigade held both sides of the creek, but this was clearly untrue. The Union forces were at least a mile further east than shown on the map.

The next group of Federals he was to encounter through the shadows were hauling artillery across the river, with the moonlight shining upon the wet barrels. They also thought he was a Yankee and called to him to slow down, until one yelled, 'He's not going to stop, he's a reb,' and fired a pistol shot in his direction.

Two hundred yards on and still at full gallop, Frank was flung head over heels on to the ground. His horse had fallen beneath him with a sudden and sickening thud. A front leg had dropped into a rabbit hole and snapped. It took Frank a minute or two to sort himself out from the fall and collect his thoughts. He wondered if he'd been knocked unconscious and how much time had passed. He lay on the ground and moved his legs to confirm he was still in one piece. Not so his horse. It was in bad way, stumbling from side to side in its efforts to stand up, banging into the surrounding saplings before falling back down.

Frank staggered over and seized its bridle to keep its head still. He could hear the sounds of voices travelling down the length of the creek. The Federals were conducting a sweep, searching for him. He had to leave quickly and quietly so that he might deliver the dispatches on foot. However, that would mean leaving a distressed horse. The Feds were getting closer. Time to choose. He unlatched the holster and withdrew the revolver, drew back the hammer, pushed the muzzle up under the cheeks of his horse and squeezed the trigger.

The shot fired and the horse's head instantly dropped from his grip as a yell came from less than fifty yards away. The Yankees were heading directly in his direction. It was time to run. The chase had begun, the hounds were close, and Frank was the fox.

* * *

Capture came with exhaustion. He had nowhere to go. The Union troops were everywhere. He'd buried the dispatches when he realized that capture was inevitable, scraping out the moist earth with his hands. Just another fifty paces on, he ran headlong into a platoon harbour. It was as if he had purposely surrounded himself with the enemy. He would have felt foolish if it wasn't for the effects of the fall and the fatigue that hung upon him like a heavy wet coat. The tumble from his horse and the two-mile sprint through the woods had caught up with him, and he felt as if he'd fallen short.

With his arms roped at the elbows behind his back, he was pushed and prodded by the end of a bayonet for some fifty yards to where a tent stood in a small clearing. In his groggy state he had just assumed that he would be shot – though why, in hindsight, he didn't know. His regiment had captured plenty of prisoners, and none of them had been shot. His interrogation, at least at first, was rather casual. He was ready to tell his lie, but they didn't ask. Instead a young officer inspected his hands, while still tied, turning them over and looking carefully with the light from a small lamp.

He then heard two majors talking, when he was referred to as the rider who had buried his dispatches. It was the dirt under his fingernails that had given him away. But they also said, 'He won't know what they contain, and the fact that he has been unable to deliver them will mean that they will not be implemented. So nothing has changed, we continue as planned.' It was an indictment upon his skills as a soldier: he had failed the task given to him, and it made him feel as if he had betrayed the cause. He just hoped that the dispatches would not be found. But even if they tortured him, he couldn't show them where they had been buried – he genuinely had no idea, due to his state of excitement and confusion at the time.

The routine within the Union lines was one of careful and quiet business. It came from the knowledge that they had secured their position both to the rear and to the flanks, and were now ready to advance. With such confidence, thought Frank, did the South have a chance, if this was a reflection of things to come?

* * *

The 250-mile journey to St Louis took a month. The Feds seemed in no hurry to permanently imprison Trooper Frank Jerome. It wasn't until early December that he was finally impounded at the Gratiot Military Prison to await transfer to a larger facility. It was here that he met Ray Nelson. Ray was wearing grey, just like Frank, but he was no Reb. Frank figured, at first, that he was a plant and said nothing. Then Ray mentioned Vicksburg. Now, thought Frank, was the time to set a trap. He'd been born in Vicksburg, and his family – his mother, father and older brother – were natives of the city.

He casually quizzed Nelson on his ties to the Mississippi port. When Ray mentioned a family named Bromberg, Frank dropped all pretence of elicitation and put him on the spot by demanding to know all the names of the family, including the three daughters. 'I know that family well,' declared Frank. 'My father and Mr Bromberg worked the shipment office on the levée for well over ten years.'

Ray Nelson replied, 'In order from youngest to oldest, it is Fanny, Nan and Sarah. Cousin Lou, but you properly know her as Louise, is Fanny's friend. They are the same age and as thick as thieves.'

Frank had been caught out. Although Fanny and Louise were older than Frank by a year, he had secretly held a flame for both of them. They had treated him like a younger brother, and had even given him kisses on the cheek for his sixteenth birthday.

Frank came clean and apologised. 'I thought you were a Fed plant.'

'No, I'm not that, but I do have something to hide that I'm willing to trust you with, being from Vicksburg.'

'What's that?'

'I'm a deserter.'

Frank assumed Ray meant that he was a Confederate deserter, and he didn't much care and shrugged.

Ray could see what Frank had assumed. 'No, from the Federals.'

That was certainly a surprise. 'Geezus,' said Frank. 'What did you join up with them for?'

'I was in New York and I got paid to do it, by a family that lived up near the reservoir. They didn't want their son to go, so I joined for him. I used his name.'

'So, what is your real name?'

'Bromberg. Fanny, Nan and Sarah are my cousins. Lou is my older sister.'

'So, you're Cal.'

'That's right, Calvert Bromberg.'

Frank looked closely. 'I knew you from Sunday School.'

'I know. I've been waiting for you to notice, although I only went a few times before I left with my father for Jackson. Lou stayed with our mother in Vicksburg.'

Frank was shaking his head as he put his hand out. 'Cal Bromberg!'

'Not any more, it's now Ray Nelson,' he said as he shook Frank's hand. 'And it's going to stay that way. Could come in handy after this war is over.'

* * *

It was Ray who introduced Frank to Mr Stanmore. He was older, at least twenty years older, which would have put him in his forties. He had been roughed up by some of the other prisoners, but why, he wouldn't say, other than he was a civilian and soldiers of both sides were unsympathetic to a man not in uniform.

'Then why are you in here? This is a military prison.' asked Frank.

'I'm a Southern sympathizer, and that's enough.'

'Lots of them in Missouri,' said Ray, 'but not too many in prison.'

'And plenty in Washington, walking around free,' said Roger Stanmore. 'But not me. I fear they will hang me for it.'

'For what exactly?' asked Frank.

Stanmore lowered his voice: 'For supporting the economy of the South so that they might win this war.'

Frank was curious. 'How do you do that?'

Stanmore leaned in a little. 'Through trade. Getting cotton down the Mississippi to New Orleans and aboard

French frigates. All payments are made in gold, and it is gold that finances this war. That's why I need to get out of here before I am transferred to Washington, so that I may carry on the good work.' Stanmore looked around before asking, 'Is it possible to escape?'

'That's not the problem,' said Frank. 'Opportunities present themselves every day. Most are fleeting, but even if you avoided a ball in the back, what then? Where do you go? You'll be rounded up before nightfall.'

Stanmore shook his head. 'If you two can get me out, I'll get all three of us away from here and free.'

Frank and Ray looked at each other. 'How?'

'I just need to get to the riverfront. From there, I can get us on a riverboat heading south. You can be dropped off anywhere you like to rejoin your units. And I can make it worthwhile.'

'How worthwhile?' asked Ray.

'One hundred dollars each.'

'I don't want Confederate currency,' said Ray.

'It will be in Napoleon French francs. You may then cash them at your will.'

'How many?' asked Frank.

'200 francs.'

'Not sure if I want to carry around two hundred coins,' said Ray.

'The coins come in denominations of five, ten, twenty and fifty. In practice, you could have as little as two coins in your pocket. But they are harder to cash, so I would suggest you take a mix. Maybe two twenties, three tens and six fives,' came the confident response.

Both Ray's and Frank's heads nodded vigorously in agreement.

'We should shake on it,' said Ray.

'So, you think that you can get me out and down to the riverfront?'

'Yes,' said Frank. 'When do you want to go? Tonight?'

'No,' said Roger Stanmore. 'I need to get word out to my contacts so that they are prepared for our arrival.'

'And how do you do that?' asked Ray.

'By paying a small bribe to pass a message to a certain riverboat captain down on the levée. Words of good cheer that seem meaningless, except to those who need to know. Money speaks sweetly in both the Union and the Confederacy.'

Frank and Ray looked at each other and had but one thought: was Roger Stanmore a spy?

FOUR

1875: GRAND LARCENY

Ozark Cells

'Does the leg hurt?' asked Sheriff Tom Kalie.

'No, it's just jim-dandy, thank you,' said Frank.

'You're lying.'

Frank half grinned. 'What gave it away?'

'I heard you cursing when you were trying to put that boot on your foot. I could hear it from up in the office'

The grin became wider as Frank said, 'You're a very perceptive man, sheriff,' while still holding the boot in his right hand.

The sheriff opened the cell door and dragged in a chair. 'I've had my own wounds over the years,' he said as he sat down. 'Got shot by the Nez in Idaho.'

'What were you doing up there?'

'Lawing. Keeping the peace. It was before the war.'

'Did it work? Keeping the peace?'

'As best as can be expected.'

'Those Indians can be a handful.'

'So can the settlers, the ranchers, and especially the miners. Does the crutch help?'

'Can't stand without it.'

'So you won't be running away?'

'Not today,' said Frank.

'OK, let's get down to business. Names of the other three?'

'Not going to say.'

The sheriff was leaning forwards and his gaze was fixed on Frank. 'I thought not.' He leant back a little. 'You got a record anywhere?'

'Nope.' Frank knew that Sheriff Kalie would have checked for outstanding warrants issued in the State of Missouri and sent off the obligatory telegram to Jefferson City, who would have sent off the required telegram to the Justice Department in Washington, who would have contacted the office of the United States Marshal.

'Clean?'

'Totally,' said Frank.

'I'm not expecting that this is your first job, though.'

'Why is that?'

'I've interviewed those in the bank.'

'And?'

'It was above professional.'

'I'll take that as praise,' said Frank.

'Take it any way you want, but you're going down on this one, Frank. Down to the bottom of the well.'

'I expect so,' said Frank. 'But I'll just have to do the three to five, then get on with my life.'

The sheriff scoffed. 'This won't be three to five, this will be ten to fifteen at least. You and your associates stole $100,000. This is grand larceny.'

Frank rocked back on the edge of his bunk. 'It was less than fifty, I counted it into the bags.'

'That's not what the bank is saying.'

'They're lying.'

'Why would they do that?'

'You tell me. Insurance?'

'I've seen the ledger, Frank. The manager showed it to me personally. The best you can do now is to cut a deal. Give me some names, locations and possible contacts, and we may get you under ten.'

'Not going to happen,' said Frank. 'It would be worth my life.'

'They'd kill you?'

'They'd be none too happy, but no, it's me. I wouldn't be able to live with myself.'

'A man of honour.' The sheriff was neither disparaging nor mocking in his remark. It was just said as if it was a statement of fact.

'Maybe I could speak to the manager,' suggested Frank, 'and clear up this misunderstanding over the sum of the withdrawal.'

'He's hardly going to agree to that.'

'You never know, if you ask him. He might want to speak to me.'

'Why?'

'It could be of mutual benefit. We can audit the ledger together and I can also make my apology for the inconvenience I've caused.'

The sheriff let out a grunt and stood. Frank remained seated and watched him leave, dragging the chair.

Frank was about to have one more try at putting on his left boot when he noticed that the cell door had been left ajar. With difficulty he got up with the aid of his crutch, hobbled to the door and gently pulled it shut.

* * *

'He said he wanted to speak to me? To me?' asked Warren McHugh, the manager of the Ozark Branch of the First National Bank.

'Yes, he disputes the amount taken. He said he wanted to audit the ledger with you and make an apology.' The sheriff half laughed. 'He can be engaging, I'll give him that.'

'What was your reply?' asked McHugh without humour.

'I said you were hardly going to agree to that.'

'Of course,' said the manager, deep in thought before saying, 'What was he apologising for? Robbing the bank?'

'The inconvenience caused.'

McHugh seemed a little unsettled. 'How much did he say they had taken?'

'Less than fifty.'

'Did he say anything else?'

'Only that you might want to speak to him.'

'Did he give a reason?'

'He said that it could be of mutual benefit.'

'What did he mean by that?'

'I think it is just his way. He does have an engaging manner,' said the sheriff. 'But the man is no fool, either.'

'How so?'

'He's confident, straight and affable.'

'Straight, you say.'

'Yes, straight, at least with the questions he will answer.'

'But he said that less than $50,000 was taken.'

'Yes,' said the sheriff, 'but on that point, he must have been clearly lying.'

The bank manager seemed a little relieved with the sheriff's comment.

* * *

'You have a visitor,' said the sheriff.

'Oh yeah, and who would that be?' questioned Frank.

'Your assailant.'

'The kid? Len, Len Aspin?'

'That's him.'

'Why?'

'He says he wants to say sorry for shooting you. Seems it's the season for apologies.'

'No need.' Frank was about to add that they'd already had that conversation down by the water trough, but he stopped and reconsidered for a moment. 'Show him in.'

'Come on down, Lenny,' called the sheriff.

Len Aspin came quietly down the stairs, cap in hand and wide-eyed. He'd never seen the cells of a jail before.

'Just so that we are clear and above board on this. I have taken a witness statement from young Len here, who stated that he saw three men ride fast down the street, followed by a fourth rider. You. While he saw you come out of the bank, he did not see you rob the bank. He did not see guns drawn, and he did not see any sacks of money. Therefore, when he discharged his father's rifle in your direction it was just on a whim.'

Frank was listening with interest while Len stood quietly beside the sheriff with his head bowed.

'Lenny is twelve…' continued the sheriff.

Lenny jumped in. 'Thirteen, yesterday.'

The sheriff nodded slowly, 'Thirteen. And due to his age and the circumstances, his statement is inadmissible. However, that is irrelevant as we have four competent and reliable adult witnesses from within the bank.'

Frank was about to ask, why are you telling me all of this?

'The reason I'm telling you this,' continued the sheriff, 'is to formally notify you that young Len here is not a witness for the prosecution. I am allowing this meeting to take place at his request, and his father has agreed to it. He has also had his backside tanned for taking his father's rifle without permission and firing it in a city street.'

Silence followed.

Frank finally asked, 'And the reason for this sermon?'

'Len is of no consequence to the pending court case.'

'That's all you needed to say,' said Frank.

'Good,' said the sheriff, 'as long as you know. You have ten minutes, which should be plenty of time to hear, accept, or reject the apology on offer. Len has practised what he needs to say. I'm sure he will deliver it in a clear voice, and when he walks out of here, he will be a better man for it. I'll now leave you two in peace.'

The sheriff's footsteps echoed back up the stairs to his office. Len drew in a deep breath ready to commence his rehearsed repentance. Frank beat him to the punch. 'Pull up a chair, Len. I'm going to sit on the end of my bunk. That way, we can be eye to eye.'

Len pulled the chair over to the bars with more than a little apprehension. 'Do you want to hear what I have to say?'

'No, it's not necessary, I think you've been punished enough without going through more.'

Len let out a long breath.

'Did your dad give you the belt?'

Len nodded.

'My dad would have done the same.' Frank smiled a little. 'It's just part of growing up. Don't take it personal. Your dad is just looking after your best interests, but when the sheriff said that you fired on a whim, don't you believe it for a minute.'

Len looked confused.

'What you saw told you that the bank had just been robbed. That's your gut, your instinct. It's what allows animals to survive. It happens instantaneously, and if you don't act on it instinctively then the moment is lost, forever. You did OK, but we'll just keep that between ourselves.'

'I wish I hadn't.'

'Don't try and wish back what's done. It is what it is. No more, no less.'

Len looked around the room containing the three cells. Frank in the middle one, the other two empty and their steel barred doors open. 'You ever been in jail before, sir?'

'It's Frank, and yes, I was in a military prison during the war.'

'You were captured?'

'I was.'

Len pulled his chair forwards a little. 'Were you in a battle?'

'I was.'

'Could you tell me?'

Frank rubbed his chin. 'You interested in what happened during the war?'

Len nodded his head enthusiastically.

'OK. I was riding dispatches for General Shelby when my horse went down with a broken leg. I had believed that the route chosen for me was secure, but the Yankees had advanced forwards with speed and skill, and without knowing it I rode right into their lines.'

Len was enthralled as Frank told the story of burying the dispatches and evading capture until he was eventually caught through exhaustion. He also spoke of his journey on foot to St Louis, and of his escape that was assisted by strong winds and heavy rains from a pass-ing tornado, and how he had been smuggled aboard a riverboat that sailed south.

When the sheriff came down, Len asked if he could have more time.

'If you want,' he said. 'Don't take too long though, and come up when you're finished.'

When the sheriff was out of earshot, Frank said, 'Do you know the name of the bank manager by chance, Len?'

'Mr McHugh.'

'First name?'

'Warren. Warren McHugh. Mr and Mrs McHugh have given our school a piano, made of rosewood and French polished. It has a brass plaque on it that says, this piano is made possible through the kind and generous donation of Mr and Mrs Warren McHugh. Her name is actually Rose. You can see the inscription when you're playing. I asked my mother if rosewood was named after Mrs McHugh, but she said no, they were two different things. That it was just a coincidence.'

'You play the piano, Len?'

'Everyone gets a lesson on the scales from our music teacher, Miss Alexander. But only a couple of kids can play, like Charlotte and Sally McHugh.'

Frank rubbed a hand over his chin, two fingers cross-ing his lips. 'I'm guessing they are Mr and Mrs McHugh's daughters.'

'Yes, they have their own piano at home, in the par-lour. Mrs McHugh can play really well. She plays the organ at church.'

'And you've seen their piano in the parlour?'

'Yes. Charlotte is in my class and we both ride together. She has her own horse. I just use one from the livery.'

'If I wrote out a note, could you deliver it to Mr McHugh for me?'

'Sure,' said Len. 'When?'

'Right now.'

'Like a dispatch?'

Frank was thrown for a second until he realized that Len was referring to his story of serving as a dispatch rider for General Shelby. 'Exactly,' he said. 'And you will need to tuck this one inside your shirt to keep it safe and secure. And it must be delivered directly to Mr McHugh in person.'

Frank leant across to the small table next to his bunk and opened the drawer that contained a small New Testament bible, along with *The Life and Strange Surprizing Adventures of Robinson Crusoe*. Between the two books was a Dixon graphite pencil and four notebook pages. Frank wrote quickly, and folding the page in two, handed it to Len.

Len seemed a little hesitant in taking it. Frank said, 'You can read it if you want.'

'Did you read the dispatches you were carrying?'

'No, that was forbidden. In the event of imminent capture, I had to bury them, which I did. Had I known of the contents, I might have inadvertently given away the battle plans and intentions of General Shelby.'

'You mean, under torture?'

'I do,' said Frank, as Len securely tucked his dispatch inside his shirt, without reading the contents.

FIVE

TRUST YOURSELF

Two Days Later

'Why in the world would you want to talk to Frank Jerome for? He robbed your bank. What more is there to know?' The sheriff was bewildered by the request.

'I want to see what he's like.'

'You'll get to see what he's like in court.'

'You said he wanted to talk to me. To apologise for any inconvenience caused. And you said he was affable.'

'That doesn't mean you can just go and have a chitchat. You're a witness.'

'No, I'm not. I wasn't within ten miles of the bank at the time of the robbery. I didn't witness a thing. I was out at Taylor's Mill discussing a loan for a steam saw. My chief teller Martin Buckley is your witness, along with three good customers whom we both know to be trustworthy citizens. They observed the whole kit and caboodle. Not me.'

36

The sheriff, standing with his hands on his hips, wasn't convinced.

However, Warren McHugh was adamant. He wanted to talk to Frank, so he tried again. 'Doc Milburn told me that he expected to see more of this – our boys, who fought so bravely, succumbing to the outlaw life. And quite honestly, who could blame them? It is one thing to lose the war, but it is another to have our state stolen from us by Yankee carpetbaggers.'

The words reflected the sheriff's sentiments exactly, and he relented. 'Ten minutes, that's all that is needed for all these apologies that are going around at the moment.'

'Thank you,' said the bank manager, 'that is most Christian of you, Tom.'

* * *

Frank stood as Warren McHugh approached and the sheriff climbed back up the stairs to his office. 'I guess you got my note,' he said.

'I did.' McHugh withdrew the piece of paper from the inside pocket of his jacket. 'I don't like being threatened.'

Frank knew he had one shot at this. 'Is that how you read it?'

'You mention my wife and children by name.'

Call his bluff, he thought. 'Then why didn't you show it to the sheriff and lodge a formal complaint?'

McHugh didn't say a word.

'It was a note with just one single purpose. To facilitate this meeting. To make you come. No more.' Frank extended his hand through the bars, but McHugh didn't respond.

Frank waited and watched. He could see that the rebuff was not out of superiority. The bank manager was under strain. It was written all over his face and neck, which showed as red welts. Best to capitalize, Frank thought, to take advantage and play his ace. 'We don't have long, so let me put forward my proposition, then you can take it with you and decide.'

'Proposition?'

'Yes, proposition. Please. Take a seat.'

McHugh sat down in the chair facing the cell.

'You and I know that a little less than $50,000 was taken from the safe.'

McHugh went to protest.

'Stop,' said Frank firmly holding up his hand. 'We're only going to waste time denying what is a truth.'

McHugh stopped and sat still, a little like an obedient schoolboy.

Better, thought Frank. He continued: 'We both know how this game is played. The bank reports a loss of $100,000 and claims it on insurance. And I bet this is not your decision. I bet you've been directed by the Missouri office, be it Jefferson City or St Louis or wherever.' Frank reached towards McHugh and he flinched, but Frank just wanted to grasp the bar on his cell and ease himself to the very end of his bunk. He was now closer to his quarry. 'You and I are being squeezed like two peas in a pod. It happens all the time to people like us. Your bank will do handsomely out of this by about $52,000. But what do we get out of this deal? After all, we are the ones taking all the risks.'

McHugh was pensive, uncomfortable, but going nowhere. Frank had his attention.

'You hope that you will be seen as the loyal servant and receive respect and be rewarded. But I doubt it. You will be seen as compliant, while I get a sentence of ten to fifteen years, which is five to ten years more than I deserve. So, the bank wins and you may think that you win, while poor old Frank gets to serve out a sentence that was not fully justified.'

McHugh was now starting to pant. Little short breaths that made his jowls quiver. Time to go in hard.

'Now, what I was alluding to in my note was the feeling I may have when I'm finally released. I'm guessing that I'm going to be angry, and I'm guessing that I'm going to come looking for retribution. But where do I go? The bank? I don't know anyone in the First National...' Frank paused, '...except you, Warren. And when we catch up, you won't be able to give me back those lost years.' Frank had kept his hand on the bar of the cell and pulled himself a little closer. 'All you'll be able to offer me is money. But it will never be enough to quell the resentment. In fact, no amount within the vaults of the First National will be enough for those lost years. So, what do we have left? I'll tell you. Just you, me, and your family to figure out a solution.'

McHugh was now shaking with panic, his hands clenched and tucked into his crotch.

'But it doesn't have to be that way. I have a proposal. It is simple, and I believe it will be agreeable. And it only has to remain between you and me, forever. Would you like me to explain?'

McHugh nodded his head with short sharp shakes as he began to cry. There was no noise, just the free flow of tears down the red puffy cheeks of a defeated man. Frank felt for him, and he reached through the bars and touched his knee. McHugh flinched. Frank said, 'Shush, shush, it's all right. All you have to do is read a statement, no more. The rest we will leave to the jury.'

His voice quivered as he asked, 'What sort of statement?'

'One that states a truth.'

'What truth?'

'The truth that allows you and me to survive on this troubled sea. One where everyone else we know is sailing by, snug and warm, on their way to a safe port.' Frank looked carefully at the bank manager to gauge his reaction. McHugh was crushed. Frank needed to provide nurture. He slid his hand under the pillow on his bunk and withdrew a piece of paper and handed it to the bank manager. 'Place it inside your coat pocket and read it once you are home.'

'What is it exactly?'

'It's a character reference. One that I want you to give in court.'

'But, but, but I don't know you. We've never met before now. How could I possibly provide you with a character reference? The court will see through such a charade and the bank will censure me.'

'Just read the statement and trust yourself. Let your instincts guide your decision.'

'Ten minutes is up,' came the call from the sheriff at the top of the stairs.

McHugh hurriedly tucked Frank's statement inside his coat and withdrew a large white handkerchief from the side pocket and wiped his eyes.

Frank extended his hand through the bars in farewell, and this time the bank manger took it.

SIX

MISSOURI VERSUS FRANK JEROME

Trial Day

'There is no doubt that the accused is a man of low moral character. He takes what is not his, he threatens the innocent, and then he runs away. This is a sorry story, and had it not been for the courageous actions of a lone boy, one so young, who through resourcefulness, fired a shot, one skilful shot, then this violent criminal would have made good his escape.'

Frank looked from the prosecutor to the jury who were all nodding in agreement. This wasn't looking good. He only had one card to play, but on glancing to the left and right he was unable to see its carrier. Truth was, he had neither seen nor heard from the bank manager after the meeting of the preceding week.

Had he turned tail and run?

Frank adjusted his weight in the chair by gripping the rail of the dock to relieve the pressure on his left thigh, while thinking, this is not going so well.

'And let me remind you, gentlemen of the jury, that this heinous crime netted the villains 100,000 dollars.' The words were said in a dramatic fashion and received the desired response of 'Ooooh' from both the jury and the gallery, now packed full of citizens from near and far. For Ozark, Missouri, this was the event of the year.

'Yes, that's right,' continued the prosecutor as he clutched at his lapels. 'One – hundred – thousand – dollars.' The words were carefully spaced for theatrical effect. 'Money that has been taken from the hardworking people of our district. An abomination of a crime aimed to rob, you, you, you, and you.' With each pronunciation of 'you' he pointed to someone in the gallery. The last 'you' was reserved for all in the jury box.

The packed courtroom immediately began to converse as neighbours turned to each other to debate the seriousness of both the crime and the culprit before them – Frank Jerome, the former Confederate soldier of the 3rd Missouri Cavalry and now accused felon of grand larceny against the State. The evidence was overwhelming. They had their man. He had not covered his face and was therefore clearly identified as one of the perpetrators by the fine, upstanding citizens who were in the bank.

Frank looked around, perusing the sea of stern faces, looking for just one, the one and only one who could play his ace. He hung his head. 'Your instincts have let you down, Frank' he whispered to himself.

'Excuse me,' came a call from the back of the court. 'Excuse me, judge. I wish to make a statement, if I may.'

All in the court turned to look towards the back of the crowded room. Frank couldn't see as he swivelled in his chair, while some in the gallery were now standing and pointing, but he knew the voice. 'About time,' he said quietly to himself.

The judge's gavel thumped twice to restore order and settle the court. 'Order,' he called. 'All be seated, and all be quiet.' The clerk responded to the judge's wave of the hand and went to the bench to converse briefly. He nodded to the directions given and walked towards the gallery and called on the petitioner to come forwards.

Frank was still unable to observe what was occurring until the clerk escorted Warren McHugh forwards to the bench. The judge lent forwards and listened. Nodding his head, he motioned to both the prosecuting and defending attorneys to come forwards.

When Frank's attorney returned, he said. 'The bank manager wants leave so that he may address the court with an important statement. I recommend that we don't allow this to happen as it just may make matters worse.'

'Can they get any worse?' asked Frank. 'Let him have his say.'

'But on what grounds?' asked the attorney.

'Justice?' queried Frank.

'Your call,' said the attorney. It was one of those lawyerly laments to distance himself from any repercussions.

'Yep, my call,' said Frank.

McHugh was a little nervous as he stood in the witness box. He put on his reading glasses as he unfolded the statement. He cleared his throat, looked up, blinked, and seemed spooked by the large gathering before him.

Frank guessed that he would know every one of those faces by name. 'Come on, you can do this McHugh,' he mumbled, 'take a deep breath and read.'

McHugh inhaled, and glanced down at the paper in his hand that was slightly shaking. 'If it pleases the court…' – he stopped, and coughed again – '…I would like to read a statement.'

'Go ahead,' said the judge.

'The robbery of the Ozark Branch of the First National Bank was a disturbing event, but I wish to place before the court and the community, observations that may assist in the restoration of public confidence and assist in the delivery of justice. The robbery was brief – I believe from the witness statements provided, it took just a matter of minutes. At no time was a gun drawn or a customer or employee threatened or molested. Clear directions were given which advised that, if followed, no one would be harmed. The money taken from the vault were funds in the custody of the bank, and it is the bank that will put right any losses through its indemnity partners. Any monies taken will not impact on any account holder. Let me assure you, all deposits remain safe. A bank investigation is now underway to increase security and address any possible reoccurrence. This has been a regrettable incident, but one that has been contained. Let me reiterate, your money is safe and secure. Thank you, judge.'

The courtroom was dead quiet as McHugh stepped down, and the relief on his face was visible.

'I wish to make a statement too,' came a call. It was Frank's assailant, Len Aspin.

This will be interesting, thought Frank.

Without waiting to be called forwards, young Len began in a loud voice: 'I have been called brave, but that's not so. I took my father's rifle without permission and fired a shot in a public place. It was a lucky shot that struck the leg of Mr Jerome, and I have said sorry to him myself, on my own, in the cells.'

'You've got nothing to apologise for, boy,' came a call from the crowd.

'Yes, I do,' responded Len, 'because Mr Jerome could have shot me dead. But he didn't. He stopped, asked for directions to Doc Milburn's, and told me to fetch the sheriff. He also told me to go home and tell my parents what I had done.' The court was silent. 'I have learnt my lesson,' finished Len, and smartly sat down.

A single hand clap began slowly from the back, to be joined by another, and then another, until all were applauding.

Frank motioned to his attorney to come over, and the lawyer leant in to hear above the noise of the clapping. He listened before saying, 'If you say so.'

'I do,' said Frank, 'but I want you to announce it, just like I said, don't pass it direct to the judge. I want all to hear.'

'Are you sure? But what are you seeking to achieve?'

'A lighter sentence,' said Frank.

'I can see that, but it may not impress the judge.'

'We'll see,' said Frank.

The gavel thumped to restore order, and when all was quiet, the attorney stood to address the court. 'My client, the accused, Mr Frank Jerome, has been so impressed with the character of the people of Ozark, as displayed in someone as senior as Manager McHugh and as junior as Master Aspin, that he wishes to change his plea from not guilty to guilty and place his fate at the mercy of the court.'

The clapping commenced again, and this time it included the members of the jury.

SEVEN

1880: THE REAL WORLD

Missouri State Penitentiary

'You got yourself parole, Frank. Half a year off the sentence of five, and it's deserved. You have been a model prisoner, and I have no doubt that you will be a model citizen.' The warden had been impressed – and why not, Frank had gone out of his way to impress him. However, it wasn't nearly enough. It wasn't six months off five years, or five off five, it was closer to four and half off a term that had started on the day he was sentenced. It did not take into account the weeks spent in an Ozark jail cell awaiting trial. The fifth anniversary of the holdup and the last time he'd had contact with Coops, Bic and Ray was just a few months away. Still, in this world you take what you can get. The warden shook Frank's hand and quickly departed.

The desk guard called him over. 'These are your personal items, sign here.'

Frank looked. 'There's a lot missing.'

'You are only signing for the items here, not any items that are not here.'

'My guns? My pistol and rifle, my saddle?'

'Sold, like your horse, to pay for your keep.'

'First I've heard about that.'

'You should have asked; we would have told you.' The prison guard was a smartarse whom Frank had spent close to five years navigating around. Now was not the time to run on to the rocks.

Frank smiled. 'Next time I'll ask.'

'Next time won't be so short,' said the guard, who then smirked as he said, 'or so easy.'

Frank took his clothes from the yellowed newspaper wrapping. It included his black felt hat, which had been crushed. He pushed it back into shape and began to change. When he threaded his arm through his jacket sleeve, he was surprised to feel the shape of his wallet. He pulled it out and looked inside. It was totally empty except for a green three-cent internal revenue stamp. This was going to be tough. He was leaving the pen without a penny. Frank gazed at the little stamp that sat snug in the wallet with its neatly clipped top left-hand corner, but was jolted out of his thoughts by being told to hurry up.

He dressed quickly, his clothes a little loose, signed the inventory sheet and release documentation, before being led out to the front gate and into the sunlight. The door closed behind him with a thud, and for a moment he wished he could get back inside, back to the familiar. But it was just a fleeting thought before he turned towards the river to walk the short distance down to the rail yards with a visible, but not pronounced limp.

The sound of the trains travelling west to Kansas City and east to St Louis was a constant source of consternation for all prisoners. The destination of each whistle blow was known, and each shunt of the boxcars an enticing rhythm that sang of the journey home.

Frank kept an eye out for the railway guards who patrolled the yards on the watch for free travellers, as it could lead to a fine, and without any money, that would lead straight back to jail. He crossed the tracks so that he was out of view from the road, and found a spot in the brush between the tracks and the river. It was apparent that this was a well-used waystation, as the marks on the ground showed the imprints of a hobo camp. From this observation post, Frank watched out for any movement.

All seemed quiet, and just on sunset he left his hiding place and went to examine the boxcars. He was looking for the chalked letters 'SL', indicating that they were returning to Saint Louis. He found a line of about twelve and checked the door on the one about six down. It was closed but unlocked. He pulled it open just a little and looked in. It was empty. This would be his ride. He returned to the small camp and waited. Around midnight he was alerted from his doze by the clunk of the wagons. Initially he thought that the engine was picking up a string of cars behind his chosen carriage, only to see its silhouette moving.

He leapt up and took off after his ride, but quickly found that the boxcar was already travelling at a good pace. He had to put on a sprint, something he hadn't done for a number of years, and though walking round an exercise yard and bouts of manual labour may have kept him fit, it had not given him speed.

It took a frantic effort to try and catch up, yet each car continued to pass him by, until he was next to the sliding door of the last wagon. In desperation he reached up and seized the iron handle, and lifted himself into the air as the door pulled open just wide enough for him to swing a foot into the opening. Now what? he thought, as he clung to the side. 'Come on Frank,' he called aloud as he inched his body upwards until he was able to get both legs into the car, then finally wriggled and twisted himself in far enough not to fall out. With one final shove against the handle he was able to slide inside, and collapsed on the rough planked floor, his chest heaving with deep breaths. 'Son of a gun,' he said quietly to himself, before slowly standing to slide the door closed. It clunked against a railway spike hanging from a wire loop, for use as a makeshift locking pin. The interior was dark and it was cold – but he was on his way to St Louis.

When Frank woke he was still cold, but the light of a new day was coming through the cracks around the door, and this offered the illusion of warmth. In the far corner there seemed to be a pile of rags. Frank was just about to take a closer look when it moved. A bearded man sat up and was somewhat surprised to see Frank. He grunted and said, 'Who are you?'

'A fellow traveller,' said Frank.

'Don't be smart, what's your name?'

'Frank.'

'Frank what?'

'Green. Frank Green.' Frank had sometimes used the name in the past. It was the name shared by two company commanders in the 3rd Cavalry. They were not related, but it did cause confusion from time to time, so Frank thought it was appropriate when seeking to disguise his presence, and that's what he needed to do now, locked in a boxcar travelling at thirty miles per hour with a bear of a man who was clearly unsociable.

The man stood up.

'Geezus,' said Frank. The man was a giant, as big as a bear.

'Give me your money.'

'That's going to be difficult, as I don't have any.'

'You're lying. Everyone has money, no matter how down on their luck they say they are.'

'Well, I don't have a penny. I can turn my pockets out for you, and you won't find a thing.'

'I don't believe you. You'll have money sewn into your jacket. I've seen it before. Take it off and give it here.'

This was getting messy, real messy, and Frank knew it. He did his best not to draw attention to what he was doing as he looked around in the gloom of the boxcar for a weapon. He could see nothing. The wagon began to slow, while Frank's heart began to beat faster. As they crossed a junction line the car swayed to the clack of the wheels and the clink of metal upon the door. Frank looked for the sound. It came from the railway spike, hanging below the inside handle.

Goliath lifted his arms as he made his move, providing a warning of the impending attack. Frank rolled to his left, out of the way, and heard the thump of his assailant's body upon the floor – but this move now left him face down with his feet pointing towards the spike. He twisted round and tried to scramble to his feet, only to feel a large hand wrap round his left boot and forcefully pull him back down to the ground. He lost balance in an instance and fell, striking his nose on the floor. It stunned him and disarmed his defences as he tasted warm blood on his lips. With all his might he kicked back his right leg. His boot heel struck something, but he had no idea what, or of any damage it might have caused. He kicked again as the hand let go of his other foot. Frank used his arms to crawl forwards and clamber to his feet.

'You bastard,' came the thick throaty shout from behind. 'I'll kill you, you bastard.'

Frank was now facing the door, but for the life of him was unable to see the spike until he realized that he was looking at the wrong sliding door of the boxcar. He'd become totally disoriented. He turned, but as he did so he felt a sharp blow to his side, which knocked him back to the floor, causing him to crumple and roll towards the end of the long empty wagon.

'I will tear your clothes apart, and then I will tear you apart,' came the declaration.

Frank reached down, his fingers seeking purchase on the top of his left boot. His thumb pushed down inside the heel as his fingers gripped and pulled. On the second try it slipped from his foot and he launched it at his assailant's face. It struck him on the forehead. The blow was of little consequence other than to give Frank a precious second of distraction, but it was all he needed – and it was all he was going to get. He thrust himself up on to his feet, and propelled his body towards the spike so hard that he thumped against the door, but it didn't matter as he wrapped his hand around the weapon and withdrew it from the wire ring. He was now armed. Frank turned, his back against the door, the spike in his right fist as he waited for the bear to advance.

In the confines of the boxcar it was like facing up to a wild animal in a cage. The danger was upon him, but Frank paused, just for split second, to ensure that his one and only chance would find its mark.

Now he attacked, launching his body forwards and thrusting his left hand up, not to hit but to seize the jaw of his assailant so that he might guide the spike to its exact target. With fingers clenching tight he gripped at the beard and pulled hard downwards as the right hand struck, driving the chiselled end of the spike towards the side of the head. The point struck the left temple, entering the soft tissue just forward of the ear to sink deep into the skull. Frank felt the palm of his fist flatten against the side of the head as the spike went behind the eye. Instinctively he pulled it free ready for the next blow, causing the head of the bear to turn slightly as he let out a roar. Frank relaunched the second blow and this time the burred end of the metal wedge entered the left eye socket.

The massive body dropped to the ground on its knees, dragging Frank with it, the bloodied head coming to rest in his lap. Frank pulled the railway spike free, raised both hands high in the air as he seized the weapon for one last blow. With all his might he thrust it down into the nape of the neck, and the body jerked violently as life ceased.

Frank sucked deep breaths into burning lungs as he fought to regain composure. He dropped the spike and tried to stand, but the effort was beyond him, so he rolled to his right and lay on the floor. His left leg throbbed with pain. He remained there for a full ten minutes as scrambled thoughts raced through his head. How he had managed to survive was a miracle. 'Geezus, Frank,' he said aloud. 'Welcome back to the real world.'

Slowly he pulled himself to his feet, his leg aching as he looked around for his missing boot and hat. He found both at the very end of the wagon, his hat crushed. He pushed it back on his head and limped over to the body and slid the door slightly open to let in more light and air. As he stood by the opening he drew in more deep breaths, then began the clean-up.

He stripped the body of all clothing until it lay naked on its back, the skin pasty white with the fat around the lower belly shaking to the movement of the boxcar. He then searched the pockets and found some loose coins and single notes. It was slim pickings, but it was something. He could find no identification.

As he was folding up the clothes, he felt something hard in the hem of the coat. On closer examination he could see where the lining had been restitched. He pulled on the thread to make an opening and inserted his fingers, and withdrew a cufflink. He felt a little further and found the second. On examination in the light, he could see they were gold and expensive. Frank felt around all the seams, but this was the sum total of the booty. He bundled all the clothing together and laid it in the corner of the car where he had first encountered the man, with the boots standing together on top. Hopefully it could be used to the advantage of another, one who would not now run the risk of being molested by this nightmare of a savage.

Frank slid the door back a little further to see if he could figure where he was. He could see through the trees that they were travelling along the Missouri River. The noise of the tracks hollowed out as the wagons passed over a bridge that crossed one of the many tributaries feeding into the river.

This would provide the solution he needed.

He drew the door fully open and waited as the miles clacked by, then as the train slowly curved to left, he saw the next bridge. He pulled the body closer to the edge of the door, one dead arm dropping free to extend out into the wind as if to wave. Frank gripped the side of the door to position himself. The train was running at a constant speed of some thirty-five miles per hour, and as it approached the bridge, Frank placed his boot against the side of the naked body. He watched, concentrating till he called to himself 'Now!', and with his good leg pushed with all his might.

The body rolled over and out of the boxcar to thump and bounce on to the deck of the bridge, then tumbled into empty space above the tributary, twisting and turning on its final journey to a watery grave.

EIGHT

LOOKING FOR STANMORE

Back in St Louis

Frank's leg and hip were killing him. Carefully, he'd dropped down from the boxcar near 21st Street and shuffled across to Market, his limp pronounced. Turning on to Chestnut Street he made his way towards the levée, resting at 8th before crossing over to Pine. Just near 4th he passed the sign of Solomon Segar Pawnbroker. Below it was the declaration *We Purchase Gold*. Frank entered to the ring of the bell above the door, to be welcomed by the sole member of staff behind the counter, a man in his fifties with a gold tassel atop his black velvet cap. His greeting came with a strong Dutch accent.

'Could you take a look at these for me?' said Frank in response, as he removed the cufflinks from his pocket one at a time.

The owner took up each and inspected them carefully while Frank studied the man's face to see if there was any hint of interest.

'You want to pawn these?' he asked.

'No,' said Frank. 'Sell.'

The man picked up a magnified eye piece and took a closer look. 'Are you Wilber?'

'No, I'm Frank.'

'Never met Deidre?'

'Can't say I have.'

'It says here, *To Wilber love from Deidre*. How did you come by them?'

'They fell into my hands by sheer chance.'

'But you never did any harm to Wilber or Deidre?'

'Nope, never met them.'

'How much do you want?'

'I have no idea of their worth, so I will have to depend on your good judgement and any gratitude that *you* may wish to offer.'

The pawnbroker smiled at Frank's approach to the transaction. 'They are of good quality, I will give you that, but gold cufflinks are personal.' He shrugged. 'And they have been engraved.'

'What about a part trade?'

He shrugged again.

'What have you got in the way of affordable sidearms?'

'Cabinet at the end. The very end.'

Frank shuffled along, using the counter for support to look at the arrangement. Most were old and in poor condition. 'That one,' he said. 'What is it?'

The pawnbroker wandered up to take a look. 'It's Belgian, copy of a British pistol called a Bulldog. It's near new. The owner found it didn't meet his needs, too small and the barrel was too short. Only good for close targets. Fifteen to twenty yards, that's all.'

'That's all I need. What ammunition does it take?'

'.44.'

'Can I have a feel?'

'Of course.'

The gun was small but sturdy and had some weight to it, yet fitted into a coat pocket with ease. Frank cocked the double action and pulled on the trigger to release the hammer into an empty chamber. 'I like it.'

'Cartridges?' asked the pawnbroker and Frank knew the deal was on.

'Twenty rounds.'

'Anything else?'

'What's left over, I'll take in cash.'

'What makes you think there will be any left over?'

'Because you want *these* cufflinks.'

'I have others.'

'A few, but I can see that none are gold. Silver is not gold.'

The pawnbroker was visibly impressed and grinned a little, so he took a different ploy and shrugged, 'Gold is just gold.'

'Not to a gold merchant, and I suspect you know of the quality from where they were crafted.'

'Why would you make such a deduction?'

'Since you picked them up, you have not put them down.'

The pawnbroker smiled, 'They are also Belgian, like the pistol. They are from a house of fine jewellery that no longer exists.'

'You've been there?'

'No, but my father has. I'll give you the gun, the cartridges and twelve dollars in cash.'

'Deal,' said Frank and extended his hand.

The soft hand of the pawnbroker responded with a gentle grip.

Frank put the revolver in his right coat pocket and the box of ammunition in the other. In his pants pocket he placed the folded notes. As he neared the front door the pawnbroker called to him while still clenching the cufflinks in his right hand. 'Take one of the sticks, I think you need it.'

By the door was a porcelain umbrella stand that was now used to hold an array of walking sticks. Frank pulled out one with a worn bone handle that bent at right angles to give better purchase. He held it aloft and received a nod of approval. 'Thank you,' he said, 'most generous,' and left.

Frank made his way down to the riverfront and found the assistance of the stick most helpful in easing the pain in his leg and keeping him steady on his feet.

He found Stanmore's office down on the levee and entered. The surroundings, once familiar, had now changed. 'I'm looking for my business partner, Roger

Stanmore,' he said, and asked, 'This is still his office, isn't it?'

A clerk looked up from his desk. 'How long ago was that?'

'Five years,' said Frank.

'That must have been the previous lessee of the property. Before us. We've been here nearly five years now. Sorry I can't help.'

Frank looked across at the steamboats as he leant on his stick.

The clerk asked, 'Have you travelled the river much?'

'Once. Worked as a deckhand.'

'From here?'

'Out of Vicksburg up to here and down to New Orleans.'

'You'd know it well.'

'Did once, but things have changed. St Louis is bigger.'

'Been away?'

'Yes, back towards Kansas way.'

'Sorry, I can't help you with your business partner. The name doesn't mean anything to me. But I'm originally from Chicago.'

Frank turned to go, but stopped to ask: 'I need a place to stay, close by. Any suggestions?'

'On a budget?'

'A tight one,' smiled Frank.

'Try Cedar Street, near the lumberyard. There's a lodging house next to The Gong that lets rooms for cheap, no questions asked, and you'll be left alone. The businesses have an arrangement with the law to leave them alone. The only problem is, it can get a bit rowdy. If you know what I mean.'

Frank actually didn't know what the clerk was alluding to, or about the name, The Gong, and he didn't ask. He left, and hobbled along the river front in the hope of finding Stanmore. He gave up after an hour, and made his way back towards Cedar Street, where he was allocated a room on the first floor of the boarding house with a view of the street. A group of well-dressed young ladies paraded by in excited conversation to enter the building next door. It was later, when the clients started to roll up, stepping from their carriages in tailored evening wear, that the scene began to become raucous.

This activity continued all night, not letting up until just before dawn. However, it wasn't the comings and goings of the St Louis gentry that kept him awake, nor was it necessarily the soreness of his hip. It was the missing Mr Roger Stanmore. Frank had just taken for granted that he would be in his riverfront office, and now that this wasn't the case, he really had no idea where he should look next.

No one, not even the old hands, could recall the name when Frank had walked the levée on that afternoon, poking his head into warehouses to ask casually if anyone knew of Stanmore, a successful merchant involved in the riverboat trade. This was difficult to fathom, as he had been a loyal Southerner, jailed for his assistance to the Confederacy through the sale of cotton to the French. A man of substance, a man in the know. A man who could arrange for passage down the Mississippi for an escaped Reb and Union deserter. A man who knew that $50,000 dollars would be in the safe of the Ozark Branch of the First National Bank at a particular time. A man who could finance four good men with an orderly plan to conduct a precision raid where no citizen would be hurt.

A man such as this, thought Frank, doesn't just disappear.

NINE

1880: REFLECTIONS ON THE RIVER

Muddy Water in the Veins

The following morning, the front desk clerk casually asked Frank, without looking up, how he had slept.

'Not too well,' he said, as he returned the key.

'It can get a bit noisy, and The Gong was busy last night,' came the response as he took the key.

'The Gong?' repeated Frank. 'What's with the name?'

'It's officially The Phoenix Club, but everybody knows it as The Gong.'

'Because?'

'Because it's supposed to have a very large Chinese gong inside.'

'For decoration?' commented Frank.

'Word has it that it was installed to ring if the law raided the place, so everyone could get out the back door. But truth is, we don't see any authorities down here at all. We guess they have just been paid off. Either that or the chief of police and most of the department are members. You get to see a lot of prominent faces if you care to look.'

'Prominent faces that like to gamble?' queried Frank, who had guessed that the club must be some kind of casino.

'It's more about the girls,' came the response.

'How long has it been operating?' asked Frank.

'About five years.'

Things *have* changed, thought Frank. A high-class brothel with a brass gong to warn the clients to get out quick before the law arrives. St Louis had become all grown up while he had been locked away in the pen.

He made is way from the lodging house on Cedar Street to the riverfront where he purchased a one-way trip aboard a small packet heading south within the hour, and as soon as the steamboat slipped its moorings and began to move out into the river, Frank felt that old but familiar feeling return. There was nothing like it, and the recollections were so powerful that they made his heart ache with the loss. He had not been on the river for nearly five years, and it was the best part of ten since he had worked as a crewman. There was nothing like it. His life on the river held treasured memories. His father, Edward, a riverboat clerk on the levée at Vicksburg, had got him his first berth, when he had just turned fourteen: a young deckhand upon the mighty Mississippi with an occupation that made him feel important and wanted.

That first job had made things easier for his father. Frank's mother had passed when he was eight. His brother Walter, older by seven years, had gone to work cattle at Fort Worth for a Mr Parsons, who had offered him a job on seeing his superior horse-handling skills at a stopover when travelling south down the river. Walt wasn't coming back. He'd married a Texas girl who had caught his eye when he trained up a horse for her. Frank couldn't figure why Walt had gone to the Lone Star State. Horses were fine, but life on the range minding cattle couldn't hold a candle to working on the river.

The job meant long hours, and the work was constant as you were required to follow all directions when told, quickly and exactly, while keeping your eyes peeled for those jobs that needed doing but had yet to be allocated. And bit by bit, the muddy water of the Mississippi began to seep into his veins, as it had done to thousands of other inland mariners before him. He would have been happy to have stayed on the river forever, back then. He would have made the commitment for life had it not been for the war.

Was it just youthful patriotism that made him join up in 1862 at Cape Girardeau? Perhaps. He had turned eighteen, and the talk was that the grand adventure would be over in six to eight months. It was in the recruiting hall that he met John Cooper, who introduced himself as Coops, and his close friend James Bicknell, known as Bic. Both Coops and Bic had also worked the river, but Frank had far more experience. They were local boys from the Cape and didn't stray too far from home. They had been to St Louis but never ventured as far south as New Orleans.

The three were tested for their horse skills when signing on, and allocated to Company B of the 3rd Missouri Cavalry. However, the title included the word 'dismounted' in brackets. They didn't get to sit in the saddle for the best part of the next three years, but they did get to walk most of East Missouri.

When Frank escaped Gratiot Military Prison with Roger Stanmore in tow, he and Ray Nelson were put on a boat heading south to New Orleans. Stanmore was true to his word and made the arrangements, getting them stowed aboard a small steamboat that travelled at night, hauling cotton down to the port. The initial plan was for Frank to get off at Vicksburg, but when Ray said he was considering the journey to France with the cotton bales stowed below decks, Frank decided to go along for the ride. He'd had enough of the war and knew it wasn't going to end well for the South.

This half-baked plan was never implemented. They never went beyond New Orleans, being waylaid with rum and Creole girls. By the time their money from Stanmore had run out in April, the war was over. Frank felt guilty. He should have made an effort to rejoin the 3rd. He returned to Vicksburg in the summer of 1865 to find that his father had died of tuberculosis the previous year, about the time he had been captured. He managed to get a job back on the riverboats, but he was now older, now twenty-one, and expected to do the same work he'd done as a fourteen-year-old and for the same wage. Yet he persisted with it for four years, until he was accused of stealing from a New York carpetbagger on a trip downriver from St Louis. The boat he was on at the time was the *Vidalia*, with a captain who had been a Northern sympathizer during the war. Frank didn't like him, but he never showed any disrespect. He just kept his distance and did his job. However, on the say-so of the carpetbagger, Frank was summarily dismissed without evidence or recourse, and put ashore at Memphis.

Just before the *Vidalia* berthed, when the crew were busy and Frank sat on the foredeck with his belongings in a sack waiting to disembark, he slipped back down to the cabins and knocked on the carpetbagger's door. As soon as it opened, he punched the man on the nose with a hard blow that knocked him out. Frank lifted the man from the floor and placed him on the bunk. He was about to leave when he saw the carpetbag near the door. He opened it and found $350 in the side pocket. On the cabin's writing desk was a half-penned letter. Frank turned it over and wrote: *This time I am stealing from you, and if you come after me or inform the authorities, I will kill you. It's as easy as that. So think yourself lucky that I didn't do it this time.* Frank left the boat and immediately purchased a ticket under the name of Frank Green to return upriver to Cape Girardeau to see if he could find Coops and Bic.

What Frank found were two men, much like himself, disillusioned and living rough. Both had assumed that Frank's disappearance from the 3rd meant that he was a casualty of war. Coops had even seen his name listed as missing at the Battle of Westport. Just one more amongst the many – and why not, as few families, if any, had been untouched by the hand of the reaper during the war. Coops had lost two cousins, and Bic an uncle.

Reunited, the three twenty-five-year-olds swapped stories, good and bad, drank too much, embellished deeds and skirted around sensitivities, such as, why Frank had not made his way back to rejoin the 3rd after he had escaped the Union prison in St Louis. Maybe they knew they would have done the same. By 1865 they, too, could see the end coming, and along with it, hard times.

Now five years later the prospects remained dim and were getting dimmer. The three stuck together, doing odd jobs and living from petty pilfering, mostly from strangers involved in the riverboat trade, never from their neighbours. They lived rough in lodgings that were not much better than a barn, but it was dry and allowed them to livery the horses and hide away any treasure gained from their crimes. And that's how it could have been, except that by 1874 it was clear to Frank that they were never going to live a life other than one that was from hand to mouth. On turning thirty, time was running out and he needed to do something, anything, to reverse the situation.

He finally made the break and left for St Louis. He had done his best to get Coops and Bic to come with him, but he had nothing to entice them. Why live poor in St Louis? At least in Cape Girardeau they knew the lie of the land, even if there had been some close shaves that had resulted in suspicion being cast in their direction regarding their criminal activities. But both decided to stay. After all, it was their home and Coops' only surviving kin, an aunt and uncle, were there.

***

Frank's meeting with Ray Nelson in 1874 came in St Louis and was unexpected. He actually walked past Ray, who stopped and called after him. He didn't hear. Ray had to tap him on the shoulder with the greeting of, 'I knew it was you, the escape artist of Gratiot Road.'

Frank hadn't seen Ray since their parting of ways in New Orleans, now nearly a decade before, and he couldn't help but notice Ray's circumstances, in stark contrast to his own. Ray was well dressed, manicured and confident. Frank couldn't help but comment: 'Nice suit. You look like you're doing OK.'

'OK,' repeated Ray.

'Doing what?' asked Frank.

'A little of this and a little of that.'

It was code for what Frank had been doing, but Ray's clothes indicated that he was better at it.

'Remember Roger Stanmore?' asked Ray.

'Of course,' said Frank.

'I've done some jobs for him. Nothing too fancy, as I'm only a one-man band,' said Ray, 'but it rewards well. Maybe we could join forces and go a little bigger.'

'To do what?'

'Depends. Stanmore offered me a job a little while back. Good money, very good money, but I had to pass, it needed a team.'

'Team? How many? Two?'

'No, at least three, but four would be better.'

'What sort of job?'

'Bank. Don't know the location. Stanmore plays his cards close.'

'Enough money for four. Five, ten thousand?'

'Fifty,' said Ray.

Frank whistled, before saying, 'I know two good men.'

'In what way?'

'In a way that is experienced in working around the law. Good horsemen and trustworthy. We served together in the 3rd Cavalry and have been pulling a few jobs, but nothing big. The opportunities are limited around Cape Girardeau. That's why I've come up here.'

'Ever been arrested?' asked Ray.

'No, you?' asked Frank.

'Not yet,' said Ray. 'But I've been close. You?'

'Kind of, and I've known why each time. We fell short in taking our time to plan it out in detail.'

Ray thought it was a sharp view. His experience had been similar. 'You could do the planning for this one, Frank. I saw how you planned to get Stanmore out of Gratiot Road. I just went along for the ride.'

Frank just shrugged. 'You pulled your weight. Always did.'

'Would you like to meet with Stanmore?' asked Ray.

Frank smiled a little. 'Yeah, I'd like that. I'd like that a lot.'

TEN

1875: A YEAR TO REMEMBER

St Louis Levée

'Mr Stanmore, have you a minute?'

Stanmore looked up from his desk to see Ray Nelson framed in the doorway, the light behind him and showing the silhouette of a second man. 'Of course, Ray. What is it?'

'I have an old friend who would like to see you,' said Ray as he entered Stanmore's riverfront office.

Frank's features were now recognizable as he appeared in the doorway.

Roger Stanmore leapt to his feet. 'My boy, is that you?'

'It is, but I thought you might have forgotten,' said Frank.

'Forgotten! How could I do that? Frank Jerome, the man who led the way so that we could escape the shackles of those damn Yankees and abscond to freedom?' He shook Frank's hand vigorously, then slapped Ray's upper arm. 'Look at us, the three Musketeers back together. This deserves a drink.'

Frank wasn't averse to a drink. It had been a long time since he'd enjoyed alcohol, and it suited the moment. 'Small one,' he said.

He wasn't sure if it was the exuberance of Stanmore, who now started to embellish the story of their time together, or the whisky. Maybe it was both. Ten years had passed since they had first met under adversity and successfully escaped from the Yankees – although Frank knew that luck had more than played its part on that night with the arrival of flooding rain and howling winds.

It was Ray who quietly informed Roger Stanmore a little later that he had raised the possibility of the bank job with Frank, and had received a positive response. 'He will know how to plan out our actions down to the last detail. He also has two good men in mind, from his Cavalry days,' he told Stanmore. 'They joined and served together, and they have some experience in relieving from the rich their burden of full pockets.'

This explanation tickled Stanmore, and he chuckled. 'Then best we discuss this proposal as soon as possible, as there is much to do.'

Frank listened with interest as Stanmore explained that a sum of $50,000 was to be transported to the Ozark Branch of the First National Bank. These were Federal funds from Washington for reconstruction projects in South West Missouri. The money had been allocated but would not be released until the start of the new financial year in July. 'Everyone knows that most of this money will be skimmed off by carpetbaggers,' said Stanmore. 'Our aim is to get there before them.'

Stanmore couldn't, or wouldn't, give the exact time-frame of when the money would arrive at the bank, or how he happened to know of such information, but he did say that it would occur in approximately six to eight weeks' time. 'Where are the other two men that you recommended to Ray?' asked Stanmore.

'Cape Girardeau.'

'Good, on the river, easy to bring up to St Louis,' said Stanmore. 'And you'll vouch for them?'

'On my life,' said Frank.

'Good,' repeated Stanmore before adding, 'Because you have just made these two men very, very rich.' He then explained how the financial aspects would work. The break-up would be in six equal parts, and even before Frank could get in a word, Stanmore said, 'My son, Dexter, will be the sixth man.'

'You have a son?' said Frank.

'Just the one. He's now twenty, and I want to bring him into this side of the business. I need a young man I can trust to provide important assistance for your escape from the law, or any posse that may seek to follow you up. He will meet you after the hold-up with fresh horses that will allow you to ride the distances necessary to get back to the Mississippi and safety.'

'Where is he at the moment?' asked Frank.

'Down the river.'

'Apart from providing fresh horses, what else is he going to do?' It was a pointed question from Frank. If Dexter was to get an equal part of the prize, he needed to do more than deliver horses.

Stanmore was prepared for such a question. 'Dexter will survey and select the safe houses where each of you will stay after the job is done. You will lie low until it is clear for you to return to St Louis. It will be the necessary security that will allow you to live your life free without a hint of suspicion.'

While the revelation of a sixth partner was still of surprise, Stanmore quickly quelled concern through the figures. 'Each of us will receive the equal sum of $7,500 in cash.'

Frank had to supress his smile. It was a fortune for just one man and would provide the opportunity to live well for a long time to come. This was more than just an enticing offer. It would allow him to once again become an honest man. It would take him from a position of uncertainty and mere survival to comfort and security. 'And the remaining $5,000?' asked Frank, who had tallied up the six equal shares of $7,500, which had come $45,000. 'Who gets that?'

'That,' said Stanmore, 'is the capital required to cover all the costs involved. I will provide that personally, at least initially, to pay for horses, saddles, guns, ammunition, food, tickets to bring your boys up from Cape Girardeau, and most importantly the provision of four safe houses. One for each of you. These won't come cheap. We need loyal Southerners who will take you in as family, ask no questions and tell no one of your presence, or that you have ever been there at all.'

'How long do we stay in these safe houses?' asked Frank.

'Until I call you all back St Louis, and I can only do that once I am able to confirm that both the state and federal authorities have not identified you and are therefore not seeking your arrest.'

'How long do you think that will take?'

Stanmore was straightforward with his answers, and his eyes didn't falter from Frank's gaze. 'It could take four to six weeks.'

'You've given this considerable thought,' said Frank.

'I have. This is a once-in-a-lifetime opportunity, but it comes with risks, to be expected of course, but nothing that isn't unfamiliar to you. What I do need is for you to give considerable thought to the mechanics of the actual hold-up.' Stanmore then smiled. 'So good to see you, my boy. We can now turn this dream into reality. We will make 1875 our year. A year to remember.'

ELEVEN

1880: BACK TO REALITY

Down the Mississippi

Turning a dream into reality, thought Frank as he watched the waters of the Mississippi swirl. 1875 was certainly a year to remember, if only through a bullet in the leg and a five-year jail sentence. It was the harsh reality that he wouldn't forget in a hurry.

But what now?

If he couldn't find Stanmore, he'd find Coops, and that shouldn't be difficult. Bic and Coops would never leave Cape Girardeau – that was their tether, the place of their roots. He hadn't heard from either of them, or Ray, while inside, and he understood why. Had they written, the warden would have intercepted and read their letters. Everything said would be considered suspicious. It was guilt by association, and if the correspondence contained just a hint of incriminating evidence, such as a time or place that could link them to Frank, it would be passed on to both the federal and state authorities. Without knowledge of Frank's release, the three would just expect that he was still inside, so it was up to him to make contact. Even then he needed to be careful, and not inadvertently implicate them at some time in the future. In fact, Frank wondered if they had gone to ground believing that they could still be arrested.

When Frank got off at Cape Girardeau, he went to the old barn house where he, Coops and Bic had lived for a time. He didn't expect that they would be there, but it was a starting point, and he hoped that the current tenants might know where John Cooper and James Bicknell were now living.

They didn't. They hadn't heard either name, which surprised Frank a little. 'Been here long?' he asked.

'Whole four years,' said the occupant, as his wife stood to one side in a stained dress with a hip thrust out to support a child that picked its nose.

'Obliged,' said Frank as he tipped his hat and left.

He walked the four miles out to Coops' uncle's place and knocked on the door. No answer. He knocked again. Still no response, so he called out before stepping off the veranda to walk around to the back of the house, where he found Coops' aunt hanging out the washing.

She recognized him immediately.

'Lordy,' she said in surprise. 'Where have you been?' As he walked towards her with the assistance of the stick she said, 'You've been hurt.'

'A little,' he said. 'I thought the walk out here would do it good.'

'Has it?'

'Not yet.'

She threw some washing back into the basket and stepped forwards to give him a hug. Frank was just about to speak when she asked, 'You have news from our John?'

Frank was a little confused. 'No,' he said. 'We are yet to meet up. That's why I'm here, to find out where he is.'

Now Aunt Vera looked confused. 'Isn't he with you?'

'No,' said Frank, 'I've been otherwise detained, in Jefferson City.' He then added, 'Just got out this very week.'

'I see. So, John and James weren't with you in Jefferson?'

'No, just me. When was the last time you heard from him?'

'Five. Yes five, it must be five.'

'Weeks or months?'

'Years.'

Frank was stunned. Coops was close to his aunt and uncle. Five months would have been a stretch, but five years?

'Guess he's gone rambling,' said Frank to disguise his concern, before asking. 'What about Bic? Do you know where I can find him?'

'We guessed he was with John, and that you were with both of them. Being so close and all, through the war and after. We did worry, you three just disappearing like that, but we trusted in the good Lord taking care of you all.'

Frank felt a cold chill run up his back. It caused him to suck in a deep breath. 'Not a word in five years?'

'That's right, not since the three of you left for St Louis. Remember? You went, came back and John said that you had found some good work and that he would probably be away for a couple of months or more, but after six we guessed that you three had decided to stay upriver. Then after a year, I got real worried. Pa said John'd be OK on account you three were together, but I don't think he believed it, either. Not like John not to get in touch.' Vera bit at her lip. 'You any idea where they may be?'

Frank's lungs deflated as he went to speak. He shook his head before saying, 'No, I don't. I have no idea at all.'

The walk back into town came with a jumble of thoughts and an ache to the left side that ran down the length of his leg to his foot. He searched for every possible explanation, but there was only two that seemed plausible: either they had been arrested and incarcerated somewhere, or they were dead. If Coops had been arrested and jailed, he would have written to his aunt and uncle to put their minds at rest. They may have known of his lawless ways, but had never been involved. So that left only one conclusion: that his close friends John Cooper and James Bicknell of the 3rd Missouri Cavalry were dead. The question was, why, when and how?

Frank now had no alternative but to return to St Louis and resume the search for Stanmore. However, when he went to pay for his return ticket, he saw the clipped, green, three-cent internal revenue stamp in the corner fold of his wallet. 'I've changed my mind,' he said. 'I'd like a ticket to New Madrid instead.'

'Heading south, not north?'

'Yes, I am.'

'On business?'

'Yes, you could say that.'

New Madrid was fifty miles to the south as the crow flies, but much longer via the winding river. Yet steamboat was by far the more convenient way to travel. Frank knew the town from his deckhand days, but not well. He had walked the riverfront a few times, and while it seemed pleasant enough, his reason for now returning had nothing to do with nostalgia. This was a spur of the moment decision, a long shot. In fact, so long that when he boarded the riverboat, he nearly stepped back ashore to resume his journey north to St Louis in search of Roger Stanmore. It would have been easy to do. He had no luggage, just what he stood up in, along with a walking stick and a handgun in his coat pocket. But something inside him said, go to New Madrid. What have you got to lose? A little time? After nearly five years a few more days is next to nothing.

The internal revenue stamp in Frank's wallet was the last remaining physical connection to the Ozark job. It had inadvertently been retained over the years through nothing more than forgetful neglect. A small, green, serrated piece of paper with the portrait of George Washington, neatly clipped diagonally across the top left-hand corner, removing the three cent numeral and the letters INTER.

The significance of such inconsequential ephemera was directly linked to a farm fifteen miles north of New Madrid and five miles south of Sikeston. The farm was off to the left of the road, tucked away in a grove of trees that hid it from passing travellers. Out the front near the track leading into the homestead was an upright wagon wheel, with the bottom third buried into the earth. Frank had never seen it. He'd never been near Sikeston, but he knew its precise location and how to get there. It was the location of the safehouse organized by Dexter Stanmore for him. The one he never got to.

The plan had been for Frank, Coops, Bic and Ray to head east from Ozark, riding hard for some eighty miles to Willow Springs where they would meet up with Dexter. Fresh horses would be provided, along with provisions for the second stage of the journey. This would be an individual journey of some 170 miles as each continued east on their own towards New Madrid and the Mississippi. The final destination for each would be their own designated safehouse, selected and paid for by Stanmore.

At Willow Springs Dexter would take the used horses and the saddlebag with the money and travel north-east to return to his father in St Louis. Frank didn't expect to catch up again with Coops, Bic or Ray until they were all called back to St Louis, which could take a month or more.

On arrival at their nominated safehouse, each would identify themselves with the presentation of their internal revenue stamp. Frank's was a green three-cent stamp; Coops' a blue two-cent stamp; Bic's a red one-cent stamp; and Ray's a brown four-cent stamp. Each had a clipped corner, and that missing piece had been given to the owner of the safehouse. Once matched, and with validation confirmed, they would be provided with safety and comfort for the duration.

Frank was not only impressed but intrigued by the plan, and had asked Roger Stanmore how he had come up with such an idea. Stanmore told him that something similar had been used during the war when working with French agents in New Orleans for the shipping of cotton back to France. The safehouse locations, along with the stamps, were issued in advance, before leaving St Louis for Ozark, as it would allow each to continue on should something go wrong when trying to meet up with Dexter at Willow Springs. It also provided for a back-up plan in the event of being separated. All in all, it was a good plan, and not one that any of them could fault, only Frank never got to carry his out. Now, five years later, he was finally going to get a look at the destination that had been prepared for him.

New Madrid still looked familiar when he alighted, and fortunately the 15-mile walk towards Sikeston was on a good road through flat farming land. However, progress was slow. Frank's leg was giving him trouble. He thought of stopping by the roadside and spending the night there, but without a blanket it was best to push on. By the time he arrived at the upright wagon wheel it was well and truly dark. He leant upon it with relief as he took the weight off his left leg, and wondered if he could have gone much further. When he knocked on the door, a man with a white beard appeared, and in an accent, asked how he could help.

Frank removed his hat out of courtesy and introduced himself. 'My name is Frank Jerome. I've come from St Louis – could I ask how long you've been here?' The man was surprised at the question, but remained genial, and answered: 'I've been here for more than twenty years. Why do you ask?'

'Well, I'm five years late,' said Frank as he drew his wallet from his coat. He eased the stamp out of its hiding place and handed it to the man. 'Does this mean anything to you?'

The man's head drew back a little.

'I doubt if you have the missing piece, but perhaps you may recall the arrangements?'

'Stay here,' he said abruptly.

'I'm not going anywhere at the moment. Mind if I prop myself up on your porch bench?'

The man just tilted his head in the direction of the seat and left.

When Frank sat, it was in glorious relief and he'd nearly fallen asleep when he felt the tap on his leg. 'Come along.'

With an effort Frank rose to his feet and followed. The soft glow of the lamps on the whitewashed corridor gave welcome, as did the warmth on entering the kitchen with its large iron stove.

'This is my wife, Iris.' Iris smiled. Frank went to introduce himself, but the man went on to say, 'You may like to look at this.' He pointed towards the long kitchen table.

Frank shuffled over. Laid upon a calico table cover was his stamp, only this time it was complete. The missing piece had been placed back into position.

'You kept it,' is all Frank could think to say.

'Of course,' said the man, who finally introduced himself. 'I am Lucas, Lucas Holm. Would you like to wash or rest first before you have something to eat?'

'Maybe just sit,' said Frank. 'It's been a long day.'

TWELVE

THE SWEDES

Daughter Liv

Lucas and Iris Holm called it courtesy to a guest. Frank called it care and comfort to a stranger. He had been able to wash with warm water, have a hot meal of potatoes and pork, and on sliding between clean cotton sheets, his clothes were taken away for cleaning. The following morning he awoke to the smell of coffee, and on the table was freshly baked bread and cranberry jam. It was a bittersweet thought that all this had awaited him for a stay of a month or two some five years before, if only he'd been able to complete his planned journey.

Frank broached the subject of his non-arrival by enquiring, 'Were you told what had happened to me?'

'No, and I didn't ask. We were ready for your arrival and waited. Eventually, I was just told that you were no longer coming.'

'Could I ask who provided that information?'

'It was a young man by the name of Dexter. It was the man I had made the deal with to provide a safe house.'

Frank sensed that Lucas was a little ill at ease when he mentioned Dexter's name.

'Have you kept in touch with Dexter?'

'No.' The response was abrupt.

'Could I ask why?'

'We had a disagreement.'

'In what way?'

'We did not receive all the money that was promised.'

'Which at that time was needed urgently,' added Iris.

'I see,' said Frank. 'I have money owed to me and I will make up your loss, but I can't at the moment. I have to find either Dexter or Roger Stanmore. And that is why I'm here.'

'I don't know of Roger Stanmore,' said Lucas. 'Just Dexter.'

'Were you expecting me by name?' asked Frank.

'No. You were to be identified by the stamp. All we were told was to expect one man to arrive after a long, hard ride and that he would stay for a period. We would provide shelter and safety at the cost of $50 for each week of your stay, with an expectation that it would be not less than four weeks or $200. At that time we needed the money and accepted. In the end it was just $50, not enough for the work required on the farm. It was a time when the price for corn, hay and wheat was low.'

If Frank had stayed for six weeks then Lucas would have made $300, so he could see the disappointment that followed. 'Did you know why I needed to come here and hide?'

'No,' said Lucas.

'Had you done anything like this before?'

'During the war. We hid men from the Yankees. Our neighbours did the same.'

'Did your neighbours take in any other men around the time I was to arrive?'

Lucas shifted uncomfortably in his seat at the kitchen table. 'You learn to keep your tongue. It came from the war. The less you know, the safer you are.' He paused for a long time before saying, 'But yes, I hear things and I have eyes.'

'From your neighbours?'

'Some, but mostly from Dexter.'

Frank leaned forward. 'When was that?'

'After you didn't arrive, Dexter came and stayed for one week, the week we were paid for, and on three occasions he went out, leaving early in the evening and returning in the early hours. I knew he must be visiting other farms in the district. He had money with him, so I guessed that he was making payments. On the third occasion he came back and it looked like he had been in a fight. He had some blood on him. Iris and Liv attended to his wounds, but it was bruising only and perhaps a broken rib. Not serious. The blood had come from someone else. He slept for most of the next day and seemed troubled. He drank heavily that next night, then left the following morning, and I never saw him again.'

Frank dwelled on the information, turning it over several times as he tried to make it add up. 'Who is Liv?' he asked.

'Our daughter.'

Frank had seen a framed photograph in the room where he had slept, and had thought that maybe it was of Iris when she was younger. 'Is she away?' he asked.

'Yes,' said Iris, 'she is in St Louis, and we miss her so. But we are fortunate. She has secured a good job attending to a wealthy family as a governess. It's a lot of responsibility, caring and educating young children of different ages.' It was said with pride. 'And she gets extremely well paid and sends nearly all her earnings to us, so that we may pay off the farm.'

Lucas was nodding his head in agreement. 'It has allowed us to expand our land holdings, build new pens and shelters, add more pigs, grow more corn. We are most grateful to Liv and the good Lord for giving us such a virtuous daughter.'

'We purchased the Benson's farm next door when they left for Illinois,' said Iris, beaming. 'It is forty acres, all fenced, and has a deep well. It is all because of our Liv.'

Frank was only half listening, still trying to make sense of what he had been told about Dexter's stay. 'Have you ever heard the names John Cooper, James Bicknell or Ray Nelson?'

Lucas shook his head. 'No.'

'If I put those names to your neighbours, might they tell me if they stayed with them some five years ago?'

Lucas shook his head again. 'No.'

'I thought that might be so,' said Frank.

'You fought for Missouri?' asked Lucas.

'I did, 3rd Cavalry.'

'Then maybe I could find something out. But I make no promises.'

It was an unexpected and generous offer. 'I would be obliged – any information, no matter how small, could be most helpful.' Frank paused before asking, 'I have to ask, why? We have just met, yet you have taken me in and provided great comfort, and now you would do this for me? It leaves me puzzled.'

Lucas looked Frank in the eye. 'I do it for Missouri, and you fought for Missouri.'

Frank nodded in appreciation.

'And these other men, you know them well, from the war?'

'As if they were brothers,' said Frank.

'Then I will do it for them, too.'

Frank nodded again, saying, 'That is most generous.'

Before first light the following day, Lucas left on horseback. Frank asked Iris if he could do any tasks that required doing, but she said that he should rest and not bother himself with such matters. Regardless, Frank wanted to contribute as a gesture of his appreciation, but when he went looking for any outstanding chores there was little that he could see that needed doing. The farm was as neat as a pin. Everything had a place, demonstrating the effort and pride that Lucas and his wife had put into its establishment and upkeep. Iris was exceptionally well organized in her daily routine, and every time he offered to help, she smiled and said, 'No, all is fine. You should rest your leg.'

'That accent,' he asked. 'Where is it from?'

'Sweden.'

'A place I know nothing about,' said Frank as he sat down at the long kitchen table. 'What's it like?'

'Cold and dark in winter, sometimes very beautiful, but also brutal.'

'Brutal, how?' asked Frank as he picked up a small knife and began to peel a potato from the bowl.

Iris looked at what he was doing. 'You don't need to do that.'

'Please, let me do something to show my appreciation.'

'Guests don't need to show their appreciation. That is for the host to do.'

'Is that the Swedish way?'

'I hope it is the American way.'

'That I'm not too sure about,' commented Frank as ran the sharp knife over the skin of the potato. 'I would like to know how Sweden is brutal.'

'It is the circumstance of being so far to the north. The snow and the ice take their toll. And when the crops fail many go hungry and cold in winter. The old and young die.'

'Is that why you came here?'

'It is. Three seasons failed. My grandparents died. My mother became sick, and when she returned to health, she gave her blessing for me and Lucas to emigrate.'

'Was it your mother's way of saving you?'

'Yes, and also helping them. I was one less mouth to feed.'

'Do you miss Sweden?'

'I miss my family. Sweden, I keep near me in this house.'

Frank looked around the neat kitchen with its white walls. 'It's very nice,' he said; he was becoming aware that Iris was not particularly impressed with his skills in peeling potatoes, so he put the knife down.

'And we have our daughter Liv.' The words came out with a mix of melancholy and pride.

'I can see that you miss her. Have you been up to St Louis to visit her?'

'No,' said Iris, 'too much to be done here. We can't just leave, who will care for the animals and tend to the fields.'

'When did you last see her?'

'Nearly five years.'

'Long time,' said Frank.

'She writes every month when she sends the money. Eventually, this farm will be hers and her husband's.'

'When will that be?'

'Soon, we hope. Liv says when she has made enough money to return forever.' Iris kept stirring the bowl as Frank looked at her, and he couldn't help but think how striking she must have been in her youth. She was still very attractive, even as her brow wrinkled, a sign that the separation from her daughter came at a heavy cost. Iris looked up. 'When you go back to St Louis, could you deliver a letter to her and ensure she is fine and healthy? I worry sometimes.'

'Of course,' said Frank. 'I would be honoured to do so.' At least, thought Frank, it was some small token of repayment.

Lucas returned late the following day with information: 'I have some news. However, I don't know if it will give you any comfort.'

Frank waited until Lucas was inside and had washed. Over coffee and sweet biscuits, Lucas told of how he had gone to visit Major Marion, the man he had reported to during the war when hiding Southern supporters and sympathisers. 'He is not well, but his head remains clear. He sent me to Diehistadt to speak to a German merchant. He knew a little, only that three men had been sheltered five years ago on the request of a man named Stannard from St Louis.'

'Stannard, or Stanmore?'

'He said Stannard.'

Stannard, Stanmore, maybe he had got the name wrong, thought Frank. 'Did he know where they had been sheltered?'

'He only knew of one family, called Platt. Not that far from here, so I went to see Mr Platt. He told me that a man stayed with them for a little, then left.'

'A name? Did he give a name?'

'Cooper.'

'Did he say why he left, and where he went?'

'He didn't know, but he said that the man had expected to stay much longer and was surprised when he was collected.'

'Did he say who had come to collect him?'

Lucas looked solemn. 'It was Dexter, that I am sure of.'

'Did Mr Platt know any more?'

'No, I'm afraid not. Except...'

Frank waited.

'He said that Cooper was a polite young man, who said he was from Cape Girardeau, which is just thirty-five miles away,' relayed Lucas. 'And as he was departing, he thanked the Platts for their friendship and said that he would return within the year to visit. However, he never did, when they were sure that he would.'

THIRTEEN

THE LETTER

Back to St Louis

Frank returned to St Louis the following day by riverboat, and this time he had luggage. Lucas had given him a well worn but highly polished tan leather valise, in which Iris had folded a freshly washed white calico shirt. It had belonged to Lucas and had been repaired over the years with small, neat stitches. Also in the valise were sweet biscuits, slices of bread, and a small glass jar of jam, all neatly wrapped in a linen dish towel. Placed on top of the shirt was the letter to be delivered to daughter Liv. When Frank saw the address of Cedar Street, he said, before he could stop himself, 'Are you sure this the correct address?'

Iris confirmed that it was. 'Do you know where it is?"

Frank changed his sceptical tone and said with a smile, 'I'll find it.'

When about to leave, Frank couldn't find his hat. Iris said that she had put it on the valise for him. He'd seen what he thought was one of Lucas' hats, a Sunday best, as it looked new.

'No, it is your hat. I have cleaned, steamed and reshaped it for you,' said Iris, as she went to get it.

As he lifted it past his nose to put it on, it smelt fresh and not stale from years of dust and sweat. Iris admired her handiwork on Frank's head, then stepped forwards and embraced him in farewell.

Lucas drove Frank down to New Madrid in the buggy, and as they shook hands in parting, pressed a twenty-dollar bill into his palm. Frank immediately felt embarrassed and went to refuse but Lucas insisted, saying, 'Take it as a loan. When you get right, give it back to Liv, and she will return it to us.'

The money was most welcome as Frank was close to penniless. 'I'll do that,' he said.

Standing on the lower deck and watching the Mississippi slip by, the generosity of the Swedes gave Frank pause to think of what had been missing from his life. When working the river there was precious time for pleasantries, it was a life of routine. In the Army it was more so. As for prison, that was the life of animals in a cage, where survival depended on instinct. Every waking moment had been one of constant vigilance. A wrong look or mistaken word could get you a crack on the back from a baton. To retaliate was to lead to solitary, or worse, a loss of parole. Kindness, genuine kindness, which is given without any expectation of rec-ompense, was rare in Frank's life. He had only known it with Coops, Bic and Ray. Without a word they had become his kin, not of the same blood, but from a bond of shared hardships and dangers. They knew that they had to look after each other if they were to be looked after themselves. Lucas and Iris had treated him like kin, and it had left a deep impression.

The paddleboat pulled into St Louis on time, and Frank found himself drawn to Stanmore's old office in the foolish hope that somehow it would once again have his name above the door. It was a stupid notion. He was grasping at straws, and he knew it.

With the light starting to fail, he walked over to Cedar Street, and on drawing out the letter from his valise, checked the number. It was not The Gong, but the building on the other side of his lodgings. His heart sank, as it was the boarding house from where he had first seen the young women walk past his window on their way to the Phoenix Club. With unease he knocked on the door, which was slow to open. A man answered, and looked him up and down with contempt.

'I have a letter,' said Frank.

'Who for?'

'One of the ladies.'

'The girls aren't allowed to receive unsolicited mail from strangers.'

'It's from her parents.'

'I've heard that one before.'

The door closed in Frank's face. He stood there for a moment and wondered if he should just slide it under the door and let matters take their course.

But he couldn't. It was a letter handed to him in good faith to deliver personally to a beloved daughter. He needed to repay Lucas and Iris, and it needed to start with this letter.

He booked back into the lodging house and found himself back in the same room that looked over the street. The one that was most disposed to the noises of club members leaving until the early hours of the morning. This was clearly one of the least desirable rooms to occupy in the building, but it was cheap, and it did come with a view of Cedar Street.

Frank took a bite from one of Iris's biscuits as he rolled on to his cot to once again let his mind turn over the information provided by Lucas. He'd tried to consider every individual fragment, and no matter which way he like to figure it, it was clear that all three of his companions had been lured away from their safehouses to meet an ill end.

The question that followed was, why had they been killed? To that, there was only one prominent answer – to cut them out of their split of the money. As for who had done it, that could only be Dexter, and Dexter alone. To have an accomplice was to defeat the aim of reducing those who would share in the takings from the Ozark hold-up. However, Dexter would not have done this off his own validation. His instructions had to have come from his father, and that was why neither could now be found.

But it still didn't make sense, no matter how many times Frank turned it over in his head. Nothing about

Stanmore had seemed sinister, although in hindsight, he knew so little about the man. Where he had come from, who were his kin? Could he have been capable of such actions? And could Dexter physically execute such orders and kill Coops, Bic and Ray?

On further deliberation, Frank had to grant that it was possible. While all three were ex-soldiers, tough men and versed in the use of guns, they would also be unsuspecting of any intent to do them harm. A bullet in the back of an unsuspecting victim from one who was believed to be a trusted comrade could be done with ease. Sam Colt had made it so, and this would make each murder an assassination.

The sense of it all, why Roger Stanmore and his son Dexter had disappeared, was now becoming obvious. Frank wondered if this had been the plan all along. Maybe he'd been spared a bullet in the back from Dexter only because he had received a bullet in the leg from young Len Aspin. Frank lay in silence until he heard the excited sounds of young women conversing and laughing.

He rolled out of bed, retrieved the letter from his valise, and immediately made his way downstairs without taking his hat or walking stick. Once in the street, he had to make haste to catch up, as the group had passed his building and were ready to enter the club. There were eight girls in all, bunched together, some arm in arm. He hoped that he would be able to recognize Liv from her photograph, or her resemblance to her mother with her white hair. However, none looked even vaguely familiar, so he asked, 'Anyone here named Liv?'

None answered.

'Liv,' he repeated, as he tried to catch an eye.

One of the girls finally replied, 'No one here named Liv,' just as the door to the club opened.

Frank turned back to his lodgings when he caught sight of a woman walking as quickly as she could in her long narrow dress. She was trying to catch up with the women now entering the club. He immediately knew it was Liv. Her colouring, her blue eyes and the shape of her face were exactly the same as Iris's.

He waited for her to draw close, then held out the letter and said, 'This is for you.'

'I can't,' she said, almost out of breath. 'It's not allowed. I can't take a gentleman's mail.'

'It's from your parents, Liv. Iris asked me to deliver it to you personally.'

A look of panic came to her eyes, which somewhat alarmed Frank. 'It's not bad news. They are both fine.'

The look didn't abate. Is it me? he thought. 'I won't hurt you. I'm just an acquaintance delivering this letter on the request of your mother.'

Liv seemed to calm down a little. 'I can't take it here, not now. Tomorrow? Can we meet tomorrow?' She hesitated then said, 'Not close. Away from here. Do you know the entrance to Tower Grove Park on Grand Avenue?'

A voice called, 'Hurry up, Lily, they want to close the door.'

Lily, Liv, Lily, thought Frank as she turned to quickly bustle away. 'I'll find it,' he said, 'but when?'

'Midday,' she called back, just before she ran up the steps to disappear.

Frank stood and looked at the black door, then at the polished brass plate, just to the right, that was inscribed with the title: The Phoenix Club for Discerning Gentlemen.

FOURTEEN

LILY

Tower Grover Park

Frank arrived at the iron gates to Tower Grove Park on Grand Avenue just before midday and Lily was there, standing off to one side and looking ill at ease. He waited until he was close before tipping his hat with a smile to greet her. 'Frank,' he said, 'Frank Jerome.'

A nervous half smile was returned. 'Lily.'

Frank withdrew the letter from inside his coat. 'From your parents,' he said, and after a pause, added, 'actually it's from your mother.'

She took the letter hesitantly, saying in not much more than a whisper, 'All my letters are from my mother, but my father always sends his love.'

Frank couldn't help but comment on the obvious. 'You are certainly your mother's daughter.'

The nervous smile returned. 'Thank you. My mother was very pretty when she was young,' she said and tilted her head down.

'Of that I have no doubt,' said Frank who had trouble taking his eyes off her. She was striking.

She flicked the letter in a tiny fanlike motion against the back of her gloved left hand.

Frank's instincts told him that she wanted to say something, and knew what it was. 'I'm not here to report on you. I am only here to deliver a letter.'

She seemed to calm herself a little on hearing of Frank's position of neutrality. 'May I ask how you know my parents?'

'We have only just met, but they were most hospitable in allowing me to stay a few days while I tried to conclude some unfinished business.'

'I hope you were successful.'

It was just polite small talk, yet so engaging, and Frank wanted to continue. 'Unfortunately, no,' he said. 'However, the company and comfort provided by Lucas and Iris were well worth the trip and will not be forgotten, although I doubt if I will ever see them again, which is a great pity.'

This revelation allowed her to relax and her hands fell to her sides, leaving the reticule that matched her dress to hang from her wrist. 'Would you like to walk?'

'Yes,' said Frank, 'I'd like that very much.'

'Your leg?' she asked looking at the stick.

'The exercise is doing it good,' he replied with a smile as they stepped off, and with surprise, Frank felt her hand slip through his arm. It was most pleasant, and for a moment he was lost for words, before saying, 'No longer Liv, but now Lily?'

'Yes,' she said. 'Liv is an uncommon name, and…'

Frank finished for her, '…and Lily affords a little anonymity?'

'And discretion. My life here is all about discretion. We are constantly being told of the need to be discrete, both inside and outside the club.'

'Who provides those instructions?'

'Ada.'

'The madam?'

'Yes.'

This engagement was going swimmingly, thought Frank, especially for someone so out of practice. 'What's she like?' he idly asked.

'Strict. Very strict.'

'But you are able to go out on your own.'

'Yes, of course. It's not a prison. But we must be back on time.'

'Of course,' said Frank, while thinking, just like being out on parole.

They walked on, the crunch of gravel under foot as Frank felt her arm tighten on his.

She pressed a little closer and asked, 'Would you like me to repay you?'

'No,' said Frank. 'Delivering a letter is a small and simple task, so no payment is required.'

'I wasn't referring to the delivery of the letter. I was asking about the price of your confidence, your discretion.'

'I've already given you my word,' said Frank, a little annoyed, 'and I didn't come here for your money.'

'It wasn't money that I was offering. Mine was a thank-you of a different kind.'

This proposal, out of nowhere, totally flummoxed Frank. He couldn't believe his own ears at the offer that had just been placed before him. 'Oh, no,' he heard himself saying, yet part of him felt like he was turning down an offer that was unlikely to be repeated again in his lifetime.

'You think about it,' said Lily, patting his arm. 'So, let's just leave that on the table for now, shall we?'

Frank was about to politely say, no, there is no need for that, but he didn't. He just kept walking in complete silence for the best part of one hundred yards before he re-engaged by saying, 'Would you mind telling me how you became involved in this…in this…' He couldn't find the right word, and started to stammer a little.

Lily let him off the hook. 'Business?' she said.

'Yes, business.'

'I was enticed. Some might say I was lured, but it was not against my will. I initiated the liaison that led to the proposition to come to St Louis.' She took in a breath. 'I have some regrets, but you can't go back, so why try. It has allowed me to send money to my parents, the sort of money I could never hope to make any other way.' She then said with pride, 'My contribution has allowed my father to purchase the neighbour's farm, and once the bank is repaid, he will own the titles to both properties outright. It will provide our family with security and prosperity.'

Frank was receiving a lesson in the greater morality of a noble cause. His brain was running fast as he tried to frame the next question. 'But the demands on you must come at a price?'

'Not really. The club is high class. Membership is on invitation only, and the work is mostly just being nice to men who would like a younger woman to give them a little attention. Attention that they don't get at home. And in turn we are paid well for our discretion.'

'Of course, discretion…' mimicked Frank.

'Yes. Prominent people prefer to keep their flirtations in someone else's parlour, we were told.'

'By Ada?' questioned Frank.

'Yes, but we just call it "turning a blind eye".'

'We?'

'The girls. It is a saying we use, when we see something that needs to be kept to ourselves.'

'And it works?'

'We keep lots of things private that we don't even tell Ada.'

'Oh,' said Frank, before asking, 'And these men are all old?'

'Older.'

'Like me?' Frank mocked.

'Oh, much older. Often with whiskers, grey whiskers.'

'And that doesn't bother you?' As soon as he asked the question, he regretted it. Who was he to judge or admonish?

However, Lily showed no concern whatsoever by saying, 'Not particularly, as long as they are polite and proper gentlemen, and they nearly all are, and most are very generous.'

'But it does involve…' he was starting to stammer again, '…involve…'

Once again he was saved by Lily. 'You mean, the involvement of relief and refreshment.'

Frank hadn't heard it referred to as that before, but guessed that that was what they were talking about. 'Yes,' he said in reply.

'I don't mind. It really isn't such a chore. It has always just seemed very natural to me from a young age. I know that farm animals think it is natural, they don't go and hide away to do it, do they? It's just instinct.'

Frank had to agree. 'Well, no, they don't,' he said, before asking, 'Do you know how long you will have to keep doing this before the family property is paid off?'

'Two years.'

'And how many years will have that been in all?

'Seven.'

'It's a long time. I think your mother would prefer you home sooner.'

His words seemed to hit a sensitive spot, as Lily dropped her head.

Frank wanted to make amends. He wondered just how old Lily had been at her time of arrival in St Louis. 'You must have been young when you arrived,' he said.

'Old enough. I was sixteen.'

'And now twenty-one?' he quizzed.

'Yes, now all grown up.'

They walked on, and Frank had to agree that in many ways twenty-one-year-old Lily was older and wiser than thirty-five-year-old Frank. This beautiful young lady had a pragmatic purpose and a forthright view on the way of the world. Had he ever been so clear eyed?

This unfolding experience of the unexpected led Frank to want to learn more about this young woman. 'You said you were enticed to St Louis. Do you still see that person?'

'I do,' said Lily, 'I will be seeing him in the next day or two for his monthly visit, but we are no longer paramours. He travels, and has other interests.'

Frank was game enough to ask, 'So, he's married?'

'No, it is business that came between us. He is a very busy man and is only in St Louis for a night or two each month. I found our separations difficult at first and did think of returning home, but when I met the other girls and saw the money that could be made, I decided to stay.'

Frank wondered if the man who had let this sweet bird escape his hold was a riverman working south down to New Orleans. 'Was he from New Madrid when you met?' he asked.

'No, from here in St Louis. He was visiting our farm when we met. He stayed with us for a little. We became infatuated, and our liaison took place one night. He said he wanted me to follow him to St Louis, and I did. I didn't tell my parents. I just said that I was now old enough to make my own way, and that I would like to go to St Louis and care for young children. I had seen advertisements in the *St Louis Evening Post* seeking young women and offering the opportunity to become a governess. The pay was quite good, though of course not as good as my current employment.'

Frank nodded in agreement.

'When I arrived, we lived together for a little while, but he had to travel, and when away I had nothing to do, and I became lonely and very bored. So he introduced me to the girls so that I might have company, as I didn't know anyone here. They were all so very nice, and once I moved into the dormitory, many became my closest friends, and that's how I got to learn about what they did and how much they were paid.'

Frank found himself flummoxed again. 'He introduced you to the girls in the club?'

'He did.'

'And you then moved in to live with them?'

'Yes, it was fortuitous, wasn't it?'

Frank couldn't help but frown, so he looked straight ahead to hide the expression on his face. What Lily saw as serendipity was clearly a set-up. 'Had he... was he...' he had to ask: 'Was he a member of the gentleman's club?'

'More than a member. Dexter is the owner of the Phoenix Club, along with his father, Roger.'

FIFTEEN

A LOSING HAND

But Go Down Fighting

While Dexter's name slipped easily from Lily's lips, it hit Frank with the force of an unexpected punch. He felt the air escape his lungs as he stopped abruptly, kicking up gravel from the toe of his boot.

'Are you all right?' Lily asked.

Frank fought for composure. 'It's my leg, it gives me a little trouble from time to time.'

'Uncomfortable?'

'At the moment,' he replied.

Lily was concerned. 'Should we turn around and go back?'

'Yes. Probably for the best.'

When they arrived at the gates, Frank asked, 'Could I inquire how much money you still need to send back to pay off your father's bank loan for the purchased neighbour's property?'

'$2,000 – why?'

Frank was surprised by the amount. 'That's a lot of money. Are you sure that you can provide such a sum in just two years?' It seemed an impossible quest.

'I've sent home $4,000 already,' said Lily with pride.

Frank had trouble at comprehending what Lily had already achieved in under five years and asked for confirmation. 'Four thousand?'

'Yes.'

Now Frank was starting to understand the spur that drove Lily to do what she was doing. As an unskilled labourer on two good legs he'd be lucky if he was able to save $2 a week after paying for board and keep. And that was provided he could find full-time employment. Yet Lily was saving the equivalent of close to a $1,000 a year – or $20 a week – on and above any living expenses. She was a wealthy woman earning a staggering income.

'What then?' he asked. 'When that final payment is made?'

'I will return home to farm life, of course, and hopefully be not too old for someone to marry me. Then I will be like my parents and have a good, long, loving life. I didn't miss the farm at first, but I do now. I miss the animals, the horses especially.'

'So you won't yearn for this life?'

'No, this has been fun, and I shall miss my friends, but I'll be pleased to go home at the end of it.'

'So, still a farm girl at heart?' was all Frank could think to say.

'Always.' They were nearly back at the gates. 'I better go,' said Lily quietly.

Frank offered his hand in farewell.

Lily took it and leant in and kissed him on the cheek. 'Thank you for my letter, and thank you again for your assurances,' she said. 'I don't want my parents to know, it would only upset them unnecessarily, especially my father.'

A thought flashed through Frank's head and he asked, 'Could you also keep a confidence for me?'

'Of course.'

'Would you please keep this meeting and my name to yourself, and not mention it to anyone?'

'Yes, if you insist. It is the least I can do.' Lily then asked, 'Are you a wanted man?'

'No,' said Frank. 'I just have some sensitive business to attend to and would prefer to remain anonymous. At least for a little while.'

'Will we get to meet again?' asked Lily.

'Yes,' said Frank. 'I think we will, and when we do, I hope that you will think well of me.'

'Of course,' said Lily. 'I think well of everybody. It is how I've been taught at home, at school and in church. It is the hallmark of being well mannered, and is a measure of good character.'

Frank had to agree with Lily's appraisal of her own character as he watched her walk away. She was that novel mix of sensibility and naivety, and it showed in her manner, her voice and her eyes. It was a temperament of acceptance, yet she had no idea of what Dexter and his father were capable of. But then again, thought Frank, she has no idea of my past sins, either. She had just taken him on face value when he arrived unannounced with a letter from her family – although his assurances that he would not betray her secret had gained her confidence. Maybe she was a good judge of character after all, as she had nothing to fear: his word *was* his bond.

Frank made his way back slowly to his lodgings, deep in thought. When he lay upon the cot and clasped his hands behind his head, he went back through every word uttered by Lily. She had innocently surrendered information on how to get to Dexter without understanding any of the implications, therefore Frank needed to protect her. But the crucial question was, on confronting Dexter, how could he extract the money he was owed and take reprisal for the double-cross and murder of three good men?

Once I get to Dexter, thought Frank, then Dexter will lead me to his father, and once I get to him, I will get my share.

However, on further thought, he wondered, *will* I get my share? It really didn't make a whole lot of sense for Roger Stanmore to do that. Why would he surrender what he had gone to such murderous ends to achieve?

Frank's gut told him that something was missing, and this forced him to act out in his mind exactly how he was going to do this. On meeting Dexter there would be the element of surprise, so he would have the upper hand. When asked about Coops, Bic and Roy, there would be prevarication, knowing that the provision of a plausible explanation was impossible, other than some deceptive account that might seek to blame others, in order to buy time.

But then what?

Frank shifted his line of thought around and quickly concluded that the first thing on Dexter's mind, after any form of confrontation, be it casual, sudden or violent, would be to kill Frank. It really was the only solution available to him, as the betrayal and the deceit had to be covered up at all costs. Then there was the money from Ozark. Where was it? Buried in a hole, secure and waiting for him? Frank doubted that very much. Or had it been used to finance the Phoenix Club, or expended on other investments? And if all this elaborate orchestration and the killing of three men was implemented to secure $50,000 for themselves, they were hardly going to give any of it away.

'Kiss the money goodbye, Frank,' he whispered to himself, 'you'll never see that again.' He swung his feet off the bed, sat for a second or two, then got up and relieved himself in the porcelain chamber pot. I should just kill both of them and be done with it, he thought as he watched the urine swirl.

A thought came to him. What if I kill Dexter to get to his old man? The loss of his son would be a savage blow, as evidently they were close, so close as to concoct and implement this deceptive trap. If Stanmore were to conclude that Frank was the killer, he would realize that he was next. It was an intriguing thought – would Roger Stanmore pay to stay alive? He might, concluded Frank, or he might turn to the law.

'That would be something,' said Frank out loud as he placed the chipped pot back down on the floor. And what if he did? thought Frank. I don't have a future anyway, not now. What precious little he once had was now gone. He didn't even have the youth to start over. He had no choice but to turn to crime to survive, to pilfer so that he could live from hand to mouth, and eventually the law would catch up with him. With every chance he took, came risk, and this time they would put him away for good, to make up for the trick he had pulled at the Ozark courthouse to secure himself a light sentence. The state prosecutor had been aggrieved with the outcome, and the law had a long memory.

He walked to the window and looked out. 'Let's face it, Frank. You were dealt a losing hand when you were still in the crib, and have just been too dumb to know it. You can't bluff your way out of this one. There is only one option left: to go down fighting.'

SIXTEEN

STANLEY

An English Gentleman

Frank dozed until just after midnight, lying on the small bed still fully dressed, until he was woken by the sound of voices and horses clopping upon the cobbles. The patrons of the Phoenix Club were arriving in carriages, amongst exchanges of bravado and good cheer. He got up and went to the window to see. Cedar Street was a lively scene of activity, so he donned his coat with his handgun in the right pocket, and went downstairs. Exactly what he was going to do, should he come across Dexter by chance, he didn't know.

Thankfully, that didn't occur.

The lobby of the lodging house was unlit, and the reception desk was vacant and bearing the sign, *Full House*. The front door was closed but not locked, allowing late night guests to return to their beds. Frank stood for a little while just outside the door to observe the fanfare. The popularity of the club was on full display for all to see, and so was the wealth of its members. All were well dressed in fine dark suits, many in frockcoats and some sporting top hats. As Lily had pointed out, most could be defined as older men, or at least as old as Frank, and all were united through a common display of wealth that was reflected in their means of travel. All of the carriages that ferried them back and forth were highly polished and shone in the streetlights, showing off their dark lacquered surfaces along with the well-groomed rumps of the well-bred horses. Even the public carriages were in tiptop condition, and, Frank presumed, charging a fare to match.

This place must be making a mint, thought Frank as he slowly walked down the other side of the street. He could smell the cigar smoke, and was able to watch as clients entered and left through the front door. He paused to take a look at an older woman greeting each, the door closing to be reopened on the tap of the bright brass doorknocker.

Frank wasn't sure if entry was on recognition, or by name, or by status. It did seem that business cards were often offered and dropped upon a silver tray held by a large man who stood off to one side of the woman and one step back. No doubt he was there to provide any necessary obstacle to entry if and when required. Frank presumed that the woman doing the welcoming was Ada, the madam of the establishment.

From this scenario Frank deduced that entry through the front door was going to be difficult, if not impossible, so he decided to circumnavigate the building and look for an alternative way in. The noise on Cedar Street immediately died away once he had turned down the far side road, which ran along the back of a lumberyard. At the rear of the building, down a laneway, were two doors into the club, but both closed and locked. One was a normal door size but solid in construction and without an outside handle. The second was much larger, with a low ramp to provide for the delivery of goods.

Frank walked the length of the lane to the end, where he turned around and started back. Halfway along, he heard voices. He stopped and stood back in the shadows to observe a patron being ejected through the smaller of the two doors. The man was clearly drunk and seeking to provide an explanation for what had caused his eviction. The two men talking to him were advising him to go home and sleep it off. The conversation was easy to hear, as the banished gentleman had a rather high-pitched English accent. No physical force was being used to expel the patron – not that there was any need, as he was far too inebriated to be of any concern other than a nuisance. However, it was being made clear that he had overstayed his welcome, at least for that night. The door closed in his face to end any discussion.

Frank looked at the staggering figure and saw his chance. It was all too easy, an opportunity served up on a plate. There was no decision or discussion required. He was going to fleece him. With only enough cash for a few more days of board and one meal a day, he had no option. A quick blow to the jaw would be enough to knock him out. He stepped from the shadows and was about to make a challenge, when the man caught sight of him and said, 'Could you show me the way out, friend? I've got myself a little disorientated.'

Frank lowered his fist quickly. He'd get him out of the back alley and across to the lumberyard and do it there. 'Of course,' said Frank, 'lean on me and I'll direct you.' This quick thinking on Frank's part would get his quarry away from any prying eyes.

'Are you sure? You're on a stick. I'd hate to cause you any discomfort.' The words were part slurred, but sounded more than sincere in concern for Frank.

'I'll be fine,' said Frank, but he found the man so unsteady on his feet that he had to half lift him on his shoulder to keep him upright and heading in a straight line.

On entering the yard in between tall stacks of sawn planks, the man's head slumped forwards. Frank was just getting ready to deliver the knockout blow when his victim lifted his head and said in an indignant voice, 'Just one bang on the gong, that's all it was, or maybe two, or three, but no more. Hardly a capital offence worthy of being ejected, is it?'

Before Frank could either answer or throw a punch, his intended target collapsed to the ground with a thump. He had passed out of his own accord. Frank, with a fist still raised, looked down in astonishment, before realization kicked in. He quickly got to work, searching through the man's pockets and finding scrunched-up notes in every pocket. This, he guessed, was the currency required to be generous to the girls or to pay for the large quantity of liquor that he must have consumed. In his wallet was more cash and a card. In the half light, Frank could just make out the name, Stanley Kemp Esquire, and an address on Magnolia Avenue opposite Tower Grove Park. At a quick count there was over one hundred dollars. 'The gods have smiled upon you, Frank my boy,' he said under his breath. Or was it the devil who had delivered? Frank didn't care which, not at that precise moment. It was capital that would allow him to survive.

He was readying himself to leave, when a fresh thought took hold. Had this also come from the devil? Stanley Kemp Esquire was about his size and weight. He pulled off Kemp's highly polished black shoe from his right foot and tried it on. It was a perfect fit.

Frank undressed Stanley, albeit with some difficulty, till he was down to his long underwear – and not once did he look like waking from his alcohol-induced slumber. When he was in the midst of carefully folding up the clothing to carry away, he realized that to be caught with such incriminating evidence would clearly link him to this dishonourable act. So he tried them on, and they fitted extremely well. He even managed to loop the tie over his head and around the starched collar, allowing him to pull it back into place, as he was unsure how such a knot was tied.

Frank returned all the money and the card to the wallet and put it in the inside pocket of his new coat. Into the right outside pocket he slid his pistol. Then he folded his own clothes and placed them at the end of a tall stack of lumber, with the intention to return once he had checked that the route back to his lodgings was clear.

With a little apprehension, Frank stepped out of the yard and walked back up to the front of the club. The crowd had thinned a little, yet no one paid any attention to him, which gave him the confidence to believe that at least on the surface, he fitted in. When he was adjacent to the front entrance, he was asked for a light from two men, both holding cigars. He politely advised that he had no safety matches upon him, and one said to the other, 'We'll get one inside from Ada,' and with that they climbed the steps to the front door.

Seizing the opportunity, Frank followed.

The men knocked upon the door and it opened. Both were welcomed in and Frank went to follow, only to be halted before he could cross the threshold by the large man he had seen before, who held up his hand and asked his name.

'Frank,' he replied. 'Frank Green.'

'Ever been here before?'

'No,' said Frank, 'this is the first time and I am looking forward to it.'

The upright hand remained in place. 'I'm sorry sir, this is a members' only club.'

'Of course, let me in and I'll join up.'

'Sorry sir, it doesn't work like that, you need to be referred. Could the two gentlemen you are with provide that referral?'

'No,' said Frank, 'I'm not with them. I'm on my own.'

'Then unfortunately, I can't let you in.'

So close, thought Frank, as he turned and walked back down the steps and moved to the other side of the street. The place was watertight and the key to entry was a referral. He needed someone to vouch for him.

Frank waited a little longer as the street cleared of traffic, except for the two carriages waiting for custom. He decided to take the risk and retrieve his clothes. On arriving back at the scene of the crime he found that Stanley was now snoring. He picked up his clothes, bundled them up under his arm, and started back towards the front of the club. One carriage now remained, and as he drew near, he became concerned that the driver would see him with the bundle under the arm and become suspicious. There was nowhere to turn or stash his clothes, and then it was too late, as the driver engaged him by asking if he needed a lift.

'I certainly do,' said Frank, 'in fact I need your assistance. My colleague has been party to a bad joke, which has left him most vulnerable. I need to get him home, without any fanfare, if you understand what I mean.'

'Of course,' said the driver, 'I fully understand.'

'If I just put these in the carriage and you follow me down the side street near the back lane, we can pick him up.' Frank opened the door, placed his bundled clothes on the floor of the carriage, then led the way.

It required the efforts of them both to get Stanley into the carriage. Frank felt obliged to say, 'All of this is most irregular, I know.'

'Not to me, sir,' said the driver. 'You'd be surprised at what I have seen over the years.'

He went to give the address when the driver advised, 'I know where Mr Kemp lives.'

Frank was playing a risky game. However, he was distracted from thinking what to do next by the sheer comfort of the carriage and the remarkably soft ride. On arrival at Magnolia Avenue, the driver offered to assist with getting Stanley to the front door. Frank looked over at the slumped body in his long johns and bare feet.

'Just wait,' said Frank as he alighted and went to the front door. It took two rings before it was answered. 'Are you the owner?' Frank asked quietly through the gap in the door.

'The butler,' said the man in his nightgown with a very English accent.

'Perfect,' said Frank. 'I have your master, and he is a little worse for wear, I'm afraid.'

'Oh, a little unsteady on his feet, sir?'

'Passed out and in his long johns. Is there a back entrance? We'd hate to make an exhibition of him for the neighbours.'

'Yes, of course. First entrance to the left.'

'Meet us there, we'll drive around.'

The unloading of Stanley was much easier with three sets of hands, and once in the house, the butler said, 'Leave it to me now, gentlemen. I'll take it from here.'

As Frank and the driver were leaving, the butler asked, 'Do I need to provide for the fare?'

Frank was nearly going to accept, but he didn't want to push his luck. He needed to act like a gentleman. 'No, that won't be necessary, let's just call it the act of a Samaritan.' Where this biblical analogy had come from, Frank didn't know, but he thought it was rather good, and would be the sort of thing someone of wealth and title would say.

SEVENTEEN

GETTING TO DEXTER

The Son of a Rat

Frank took the carriage back to Cedar Avenue, saying that he needed to return to the club. He paid for the fare with two of Stanley's dollar bills, which made for a healthy tip in an effort to keep the driver's silence, while saying, 'Best we keep this just between ourselves.'

'That's not a problem. Those who can indulge, usually do,' he replied in a matter-of-fact way, before adding, 'I'd do the same if I could.'

Frank was taken by these words of wisdom, and responded with a little of his own insight into life by saying, 'Too true. I guess we are all susceptible to sin.'

'No, not sins, just misdemeanours mostly. Mr Kemp uses my carriage often, and apart from being a gentleman, he has always been generous, like yourself.'

Frank now wondered if he had been too smart for his own good by entering into a personal conversation. The driver could provide a direct link between himself and Stanley. So with a little quick thinking, which seemed to be the order of the day, he said, 'I only just met him tonight, briefly, but he did seem to be a most pleasant fellow.' On saying the words 'most pleasant fellow', he wondered if he was getting a little carried away at playing the part of a moneyed gentleman. He'd never referred to anyone as being a 'most pleasant fellow' before.

'He is,' said the carriage driver, 'If only there were more like him, and yourself, sir. Willing to help others.'

As the carriage departed, Frank looked down at Stanley's evening attire that he was now wearing. Why is it, he thought, that tailored fabric can change not just the physical appearance of a man, but also the perception of his character? He was learning fast, albeit a little late, that refinement and money matter, and lots of money matters most of all.

Frank woke late from his adventures and was able to afford a full breakfast of ham, eggs, cornbread and coffee. With hands cupped around the enamel mug he considered what next to do. Lily had been expecting to see Dexter in the next day or two, which was now either today or tomorrow. There was little time to make his move. He thought of going back to Lily for more information on when Dexter might enter or leave the club. However, he quickly dismissed this as being foolish, as it would put Lily at risk. He would try to get in again tonight.

The question was, how?

Maybe he could befriend an acquaintance outside the club to vouch for him at the door. On further consideration this seemed improbable. Who vouches for someone they have only just met? He could try and enter with a group, yet this was foiled on his first attempt. The thought occurred to him that maybe he could make an acquaintance outside the club, then try and enter a little later using that name to say that he had an urgent message. If asked what the message was so that it could be delivered, Frank could say it was personal and that he needed to deliver it in person.

Deep in thought, he sipped from the mug. It was a flimsy plan at best, and downright silly at worst. It was like play acting, and he was no actor. Any of one hundred different little queries could shatter the illusion not only of his false message, but also of his fake identity as Frank Green. No matter how many times or perspectives Frank used to find a sound solution, nothing came to mind. The one thing he knew for sure, was that he was willing to try anything to get to Dexter.

Frank returned to his lodgings and cleaned his pistol, stripping it down by removing the cylinder and wiping each part clean. He also pulled through the 2½ in long barrel prior to testing the double action to confirm that it was functioning as it should. Finally he wiped clean each of the five .44 rounds, which he returned to their chambers once the gun was reassembled. It was ready. He was ready. All that was now needed was a moment with Dexter, and fate could do as it wanted.

Frank skipped lunch, not feeling hungry after his full breakfast, and around mid-afternoon, he went for a shave and haircut. That evening he dined on a bowl of beef stew around six. On returning to his lodgings he rested and waited until the traffic started to fill Cedar Road with patrons of the club. By ten it was a hive of activity as Frank dressed in Stanley's suit and went downstairs.

He felt comfortable in his stolen clothes and the persona they furnished. His walking stick also seemed to add to the stature of being a wealthy gentleman. As he moved about, he was also well aware that he raised no suspicion, being accepted as one in a crowd of peers. His first attempt to strike up a friendship and develop some sort of tenuous relationship was cut short when the man he was talking to, excused himself as his carriage had arrived. Frank had picked the wrong man. He needed someone who was going into the club, not leaving. The second attempt seemed to be going well as the conversation turned to service in the Missouri military, until he felt a tap on his shoulder. He turned to see the carriage driver from the previous night standing behind him. Frank was alarmed, but remained calm and ready to deal with this predicament on its merits. The carriage driver smiled and tilted his head. Frank looked in the indicated direction and saw Stanley, pushing through the crowd. Keeping calm was one thing, he now needed to keep his nerve.

Frank had no idea what to say, and quickly wondered if retreat was the best option, to become lost in the mob and skulk away. But it was now too late, and he'd have to bluff – but just as he was about to open his mouth, Stanley beat him to the punch.

'Is this the man? The good Samaritan who came to my aid in my hour of need?'

'It is,' said the carriage driver.

Thrusting out a hand, he introduced himself: 'Stanley Kemp. It seems we met last evening, but forgive me, I really can't recall. Had a little bit too much to drink. I don't think you got to see me at my best.'

'Frank. Frank Green.'

Stanley passed a five-dollar bill to the carriage driver who seemed well pleased with his work. 'Well, Frank Green, shall we go in?'

Could it be this easy? thought Frank. 'Certainly,' he heard himself say. 'I'd like that, but you will have to vouch for me, as I'm not a member.'

'No trouble at all.' Stanley sounded confident.

Frank followed him up the steps to stand behind a group of three who were being questioned. They passed the test with ease and were welcomed in. Now it was their turn. Stanley led the way and went to pass, only to be stopped abruptly. Two steps down, Frank was unable to see or hear what was being said, but it was clear that they had met an immovable object in the form of Ada, and were going nowhere. The seconds ticked by, and commenced to make minutes. He glanced around Stanley's left side to see the largish woman with a scowl on her face, which indicated that the conversation was not going well.

The door closed abruptly.

Stanley turned to Frank, who asked, 'What happened?'

'Bit of a hiccup, I'm afraid. I'm on the banned list for twenty-four hours – seems I upset some of the other members last night with my antics. I'm told that I also broke some objects. I said I'd pay, but was told that this time I wouldn't be able to buy my way out of my penance.' Frank went to speak, but it seemed that Stanley had not yet finished. 'What do you say we re-group at the Planter's on Fourth and Pine? They have an excellent bar there, better than the Phoenix. Trouble is, it doesn't have the charms of the ladies, but it will give me the opportunity to express my thanks.'

Frank now needed to run the course: if he could get in tomorrow night, he should still have a chance of confronting Dexter. He agreed to the invitation, and was about to learn that his host was one of the most talkative men in Missouri – maybe the whole South.

Stanley Kemp was a man of many words on just about every subject imaginable. On the trip up to the Planter's, Stanley spoke about his time at Oxford where he studied mathematics, rowed boats, played rugby and chased the local girls around the village greens. He told of how he had entered his family's business as an importer of fine French wine, and how his father had become involved in the procurement of cotton for the mills in England, initially via France, during the height of the Civil War. This had led the family to invest in the South at the end of the war, choosing tobacco and cotton.

Slowly, where he could get a word in, Frank turned the conservation back to the club, so that he might get an understanding as to its layout and operation, but each time Stanley would point the conversation in a different direction. In the end, Frank just decided to let it go and enjoy his whisky, topping up his glass with chilled water so that it didn't go to his head after so many years of abstinence.

And all the time, this one-sided exchange continued to drift in and out of topics, events and various subjects. Most were of little to no interest to Frank, however, they saved him from direct questions about his own past. It was only when Stanley started talking about how his father had sent him to St Louis, some four years ago, to look after business interests, and in particular the trade of cotton, that the name Stannard came up.

Frank said, 'Stannard, I've heard that name somewhere before.'

'I'm sure you have, the Democrat Senator for Missouri, Roger Stannard. Wonderful man, helped get all that cotton out through New Orleans during the war.'

'Stannard or Stanmore?' asked Frank.

'No, Stannard, big wheel now.'

'Where is he located?' asked Frank.

'Washington of course.'

Frank couldn't shake off the feeling that they were talking about the same man. 'How long has he been there?'

'All the time I've been in St Louis, so at least four years.'

'Do you know him well?'

'Not well, I know his son better, much better.'

'And who's he?' asked Frank, pouring a little more water into his glass.

'Dexter Stannard of course, the owner of the Phoenix Club.'

Frank spilt a little water and had to steady himself. He immediately recalled that Lucas had used the name Stannard, after he had spoken to a German merchant in Diehistadt when seeking information on Coops, Bic and Ray. 'His son is here in St Louis?' he asked gently.

'Yes, I believe he arrived last night and will be departing tomorrow.'

Frank couldn't contain himself. 'What time tomorrow?'

'Oh, late. I'll see him tomorrow before he goes and smooth over this misunderstanding. That's what I said to Ada, and she knows I'll win. She'll let us in tomorrow. She just wanted to show who's the boss while Dexter is here.'

Frank was quietly filling his lungs with air to settle himself as he asked, 'So, Dexter travels?'

'Constantly, he has business interests up and down the Mississippi. A very handy man to know. He only gets up to the club once a month to collect the takings and ferry the money back to his father.'

Frank now knew how a miner felt when his pick strikes gold. 'I would like to meet him,' said Frank hoping that the words didn't sound sinister.

'And so you shall,' said Stanley, 'when we make you a member of the club tomorrow evening. Mind you, it's an expensive association to belong to, I've spent a fortune there over the last few years, no wonder it is so darn profitable.'

'How profitable?' asked Frank cautiously.

Stanley finished his glass of champagne and asked for another. 'And another whisky for Frank as well.'

'Profitable?' Frank had to ask again.

Stanley lent in close and said quietly, 'Very. They are clearing $50,000 a month nett, which is what it cost him and his father to set it up initially, and that was nearly five years ago. So, the club is now producing the equivalent of the set-up capital in profit, every month.'

'A gold mine,' suggested Frank.

'Better,' said Stanley as he leant in a little closer to pass on some more tantalizing and confidential information. 'No wonder his father is getting things done in Washington. A politician with deep pockets can work wonders. He can buy favours to achieve favourable results, and he also heads up the senate committee on banking. Very influential. This father and son team are going to be two of the wealthiest men in the nation, just mark my words.'

Frank was willing to push his luck with his questioning. He was getting too close not to. 'How do you get $50,000 from St Louis to the Washington?'

Stanley lent back and sipped from his glass. 'In a carpetbag. No one pays any notice. Dexter told me that he was once asked by some Yankees, when travelling by train, what he had in the bag between his feet, and he said $50,000 in cash. Of course, they didn't believe him. They just laughed, and asked where you could get money like that, and he said, "Initially, from a bank".'

EIGHTEEN

A FAIRYTALE

Caught with His Pants Down

Frank's stomach churned for most of the next day. When he had excused himself from Stanley's company at the bar of the Planter's the night before, it was not before he had received a firm arrangement to meet the following evening at eight at the front of the club. Now his mind was sifting through every possibility to distil the key ingredients that would lead to a confrontation with Dexter – and all the while his gut twisted tight.

The results of his deliberations came to this: first and foremost, he had to get inside the club. Second, he had to find Dexter. Third, came a new priority: Frank wanted the money, the fifty thousand in the carpetbag. How he was going to pull that off he didn't know, other than offering the threat of imminent death. Fourth, he would avenge the deaths of Coops, Bic and Ray. Once again, he didn't know how he would do this. Pulling a trigger in cold blood was not something he had ever done. Killing during the war had been in battle to seize and hold ground. In the boxcar it was a fight for survival. This was different, it would be murder, but it had to be done. Three had been murdered, and Frank was now intending to serve the same sentence back upon Dexter. Yet he wasn't sure if he could actually do it.

On meeting up with Stanley, a surprising but not unfamiliar sensation returned to him, one that he had first encountered just prior to advancing into battle as a young soldier. The feeling was a mix of concern and relief. Concern at the possibility of failure and the consequences that follow, and relief that the end was in sight regardless of the outcome.

All the moves had been rehearsed over and over and over in his head. He knew from experience that they would stick. Now he just had to do it, to physically act out each planned step. And as soon as he began to mount the steps to the front door of the Phoenix Club with the loaded revolver in the pocket of his coat, he became calm.

Stanley led the way once again and was recognized. Some words of warning were passed from the keeper of the door, the same man Frank had seen previously. He was reminding the returning recalcitrant of the need to be on best behaviour. Stanley gave a solemn undertaking and stepped over the threshold.

Frank followed, to be greeted by an exceedingly spacious entrance with a white marble floor, and there in pride of place, hanging off a large rosewood frame, was a giant Chinese gong. Alongside the highly polished brass disc, with a dragon embossed upon its face, hung a large mallet. The one that had been used by Stanley in his moment of drunken merriment to wake up the neighbours and send the false warning that the law was on its way.

Stanley glanced back and said, 'Follow me. Best we pow-wow with the chief first.' He led Frank to a door off to one side of the main staircase, marked with the title of *Bureau* in gold leaf. 'I'll introduce you to Ada. She can be rather scary, but best to stay on her good side. She's the power behind the throne.' Stanley knocked on the door.

'Enter,' came the abrupt reply.

'Here goes,' said Stanley, who on opening the door immediately engaged in a warm greeting. 'Ada, it's Stanley and I've come to apologise once again for my unruly behaviour the other evening, and to introduce you to Frank Green, who wishes to become your newest member.'

Ada was sitting at a desk facing the side wall. The sour look that greeted Frank came with a degree of menace mixed with contempt.

Before Frank could say anything, she said to Stanley abruptly, 'Are you vouching for him?'

'I am.'

'Is he English?'

'No,' said Frank. 'From Vicksburg.'

'What business are you in?' Once again it was curt, her manner reminding Frank of a prison guard. 'Riverboats,' he lied.

Ada was asking the questions that Stanley never got around to, and it showed on his face. 'Riverboats,' he said, 'most interesting.'

Ada picked up on it immediately. 'Have you two known each other long?'

'Long enough to be like brothers,' said Frank. 'We look out for each other, especially if we get into a little trouble.'

Stanley quickly fell into line by eagerly saying, 'Brothers, absolutely. To keep each other out of trouble.'

Ada opened the bottom drawer of the desk and lifted out a sheet of paper. 'This is the application form, and I will require $50 as a joining fee on acceptance. You are free to use the facilities this evening, but only for this evening, until you are accepted as a member.'

Frank took the form, saying, 'That's all the time I will need to decide if I would like to join.'

Ada seemed to take umbrage at the comment. 'We have no trouble filling our membership requirements. And our clientèle is amongst the most wealthy and important of St Louis.'

Frank was looking beyond the form towards the floor where he could see a carpetbag beside the desk and next to the safe, the door slightly ajar to show that it was not locked. 'Excellent,' he said.

Ada saw where he had been looking and stood up to position herself between the bag and Frank, saying, 'Just slide the application under the door before you leave.'

'Of course,' said Frank.

'I believe Dexter is in tonight,' said Stanley. 'I'd like to pay my respects. Where will I find him?'

'He's indisposed,' said Ada.

Stanley nodded politely. 'I understand,' he said, 'maybe later.'

'He's leaving this evening on the late-night riverboat to New Orleans. I doubt if he will have time.'

'Pity,' said Stanley. 'I just wanted to give him my assurance that I'll be on best behaviour.'

'I'll pass it on,' said Ada. She was keen to get them out of her office.

On leaving, Stanley said, 'I think that worked rather well. Smoothed over the ruffled feathers.' He sucked in a deep breath. 'Where to now? Of course, the girls and champagne.'

'I might just go for a wander,' said Frank.

'Would you like me to come with you and show you the sights? The bar, the gaming tables?' asked Stanley.

'No, that won't be necessary, I won't be long. Where can I join you?'

'I'll be upstairs, in one of the suites.'

'Any in particular?' asked Frank.

'Any but Suite A. I'll leave the door ajar so that you may find us. I'll organize the girls.'

As Stanley commenced to climb the stairs Frank called, 'Why not Suite A?'

'Dexter will be using it. When he's in town, he always uses Suite A. It's kept reserved for him. It's the biggest and grandest.'

Frank stood quietly at the bottom of the staircase that curved graciously up to the mezzanine floor above, his eyes following Stanley to the top. He waited for a minute while folding the application form and placing it inside his coat pocket, and then followed three men as they climbed the stairs. He positioned himself to use them as a shield, to remain hidden from view.

The mezzanine formed a large oval, bounded by an ornate balustrade from which to lean on when looking back down to the entrance way, while on the wall side was a series of doors, each with a letter in gold. On arriving at the top step, Frank was able to see two wide passage-ways leading east and west to more suites. He continued on behind his shield as they advanced towards the foyer between the two passages. When adjacent to Suite E, he caught sight of two women a little way ahead. One turned side on.

It was Lily.

Frank froze, then quickly stepped back behind the three men and turned away as if to examine the opulence that surrounded him – the long red velvet curtains, red carpet and cream walls. Sheepishly, he looked back. 'Don't look this way,' he said to himself as Lily gave a little wave to someone approaching. Frank half turned to see who she was gesturing to. It was Stanley, who joined her. They spoke for only a matter of seconds, before Lily, Stanley and another young woman entered Suite C, leaving the door partly open.

Frank turned and walked back around the full length of the mezzanine to approach Suite A from the other side, to avoid passing the door left open by Stanley. When he was within half-a-dozen steps, he steeled himself and slid his right hand into his coat pocket to wrap his fingers around the pistol grip of the revolver. A sign hung from a hook on the door advising that a private party was in progress and not to disturb. Frank slowly turned the door handle with his left hand and felt it open, making an audible click. He held the handle and his breath, then slowly eased it open.

It was dark.

Frank stepped into a passageway that led to a closed black curtain. He closed the door gently behind him, and all became pitch black. He stood still and closed his eyes in an effort to gain some night vision, as just beyond the curtain he could clearly hear the sounds of physical exertion. He edged forwards and carefully parted the heavy drape to look in. The light in the room was red and dim. He separated the curtain a little more and could see the silhouette of a standing figure as he thrust his hips forwards towards the buttocks of a woman, bent forwards and holding on tight to the seat of a chair. Frank closed his eyes and counted to five, to better allow his vision to adapt to the poor light. The woman's erotic moans were now accompanied by the grunts of the male. Frank looked again and could see the profile of a man he assumed must be Dexter.

He stepped sideways through the fabric screen, then carefully edged along the back wall, slowly, until he was directly behind the couple. He paused and observed for a moment or two as he withdrew the pistol from his coat pocket. With care he moved towards Dexter.

When just one pace behind him, he lifted the hand-gun towards the back of Dexter's neck and firmly pressed the end of the cold barrel to the skin behind the ear. 'Is it Dexter Stannard, or Dexter Stanmore?' said Frank. 'Because I'm kind of confused.'

Dexter gave a jolt and immediately stopped his gyra-tions, pushing the woman away, causing her to tumble on to the floor with a thump, accompanied by an unla-dylike expletive.

'Yes, it's me, Frank, and I've come for our money. Mine, Coops, Bic and Ray.'

Dexter went into a state of shock, his mouth moving but not a sound passing his lips. The young lady was still on the floor, rearranging her under garments in a flurry with eyes wide.

'Just stay where you are for the moment and rest after all the exertion,' said Frank, 'and you'll be just fine. This is between me and your boss. He owes me some money, and I've come to collect. Do you understand?'

The woman nodded her head vigorously.

'Good,' said Frank. 'So, no need to make a fuss. Just remain discreet and turn a blind eye.'

The woman nodded her understanding again as Dexter croaked out in a faulting voice, 'Coops, Bic and Ray got their money, and I'll get you yours. I just don't have it on me, but I have some of it down in the office. It will just take a little time to raise the rest.'

Dexter was gathering his thoughts and stalling for time, and it was exactly what Frank had expected.

The fairytale continued. 'I don't keep that sort of money around, Frank. It's a lot of money and will take time to raise. If you can just wait a little.'

'I'm sick of waiting, Dexter. If you can't give it to me, then best I shoot you now and be done with it.' Frank drew the hammer back on the pistol and with each click, Dexter's head jerked.

'Some, I can give you some. In good faith, and I can get the rest to you tomorrow, when the bank opens.'

Lies, thought Frank, and he had to stop the urge to squeeze the trigger. Good faith? Had it been good faith that lured his three close companions to their deaths? Dexter's deceit was masking his treachery, and Frank knew that he now needed to be on guard for any devious ploy to take back the advantage. 'Pull up your trousers, nice and easy, and we'll go and get what you've got in the office.'

'Yes, we'll go downstairs and sort this out.' Dexter was regaining his composure.

Frank knew he was scheming, and said, 'I'll tell you how this is going to work. You will walk one pace ahead. I will be directly behind with this gun in my pocket and my hand on the grip. If anything goes wrong I'll shoot you in the back, then I'll shoot you in the head. It's as simple as that. I will kill you. Understand?'

'Yes, I understand, Frank.' The words were now steady and coherent. A sign of returning self-control.

Frank wasn't buying any of Dexter's assurances, he just said, 'Good. This will only take a matter of minutes and then you won't see me again.'

'Sure, sure, Frank,' said Dexter, accepting the proposal with enthusiasm. 'I'll lead, you follow.'

Frank felt his hand tighten on the pistol grip.

NINETEEN

LILY, LILY

Fire, Fire, Fire!

As they started to descend the stairs, Dexter glanced back at Frank, then cast his eyes quickly away. Frank knew what he was thinking, he'd seen the walking stick.

On arriving at the office door, Dexter went to knock. Frank told him to enter. Ada looked up and on seeing Dexter, smiled, only to then recognize Frank and respond with a scowl. Frank closed the door behind him and pulled the revolver from his pocket. Ada recoiled with surprise, but only for a second or two, before her eyes narrowed in contempt.

'How much do we have in the safe, Ada?' said Dexter.

Ada seemed at a loss as how to answer.

'The safe, Ada, how much do we have in the safe?'

'Just the safe?' she said hesitantly.

'Yes, the safe. How much do we have in the safe?'

Frank remained expressionless as he watched this foolish charade being played out for his benefit.

Ada gave a cough. 'Ah, well, we have, I think,' she gave another cough, 'two thousand dollars.'

'Would you please take it out and give it to this man.'

'All of it?' she inquired.

'Yes, all that is in the safe.'

Ada bent forwards from her chair, opened the safe door and removed a cash box. Lifting the tin lid, a display of notes could be seen in the closest row of separated compartments. The other compartments were all empty. It told Frank that the money from the safe had been placed in the carpetbag for Dexter's departure.

'Now hand it to this man, so that he may leave peaceably.'

'All of it?' asked Ada.

'All of it,' said Dexter.

Ada collected the notes together, and with two hands lifted them forwards towards Frank, as if in some kind of religious offering.

'I will need something to carry it in,' said Frank. 'I don't have anything,' said Ada. 'Just put it in your pockets.'

Ada and Dexter were kindred spirits, devious and greedy to the core. To take the money would require him to remove his hand from the walking stick. Frank held his tongue. Even with a gun to his back, Dexter was trying to orchestrate a betrayal, while hiding fifty thousand dollars in the carpetbag at his feet. Feelings of anger were beginning to rise in Frank. Dexter wasn't even going to let him leave with the lousy petty cash from this money-making machine called the Phoenix Club.

'Put it in the carpetbag with the fifty thousand,' said Frank.

They both remained motionless for a moment, before Ada dropped the bundle of notes from her hands to distract Frank as she swivelled in her chair, pulled open the top desk drawer and seized a revolver lying on its side in plain view. Her hand lifted with speed and agility towards Frank, the barrel raised, the threat imminent – but with his pistol pressed to Dexter's back, he didn't have a clear line of fire to retaliate. Instinctively he thrust out his walking stick in an attempt to strike the weapon from her hand, just as a shot exploded with a boom in the confines of the small room.

Frank felt his walking stick kick back in his hand as the bullet snapped the staff in two.

Dexter immediately let out a grunt and folded forwards towards Ada as he gripped at the desk. She twisted the revolver in Frank's direction for a second shot.

Still unable to get a clear line, Frank thrust the stem of his walking stick at Ada and the jagged, splintered end struck her in the windpipe. Her head jerked back just as a second shot flashed before Frank's eyes.

The muzzle of Ada's handgun was so close to Frank that he felt the blast and tasted the acrid smoke from the burnt powder. He was sure a wound must follow, but the bullet passed between him and Dexter to strike and shatter a lamp on a small table against the rear wall near the door, causing additional chaos to the unfolding turmoil and confusion. The spattered oil now ignited with a whoosh, flaring into a brilliant light that filled the room from a ball of flame that mushroomed to the ceiling.

Ada slumped back in her chair with blood pumping from the wound to her neck, while Dexter continued to clutch the desktop in an effort to remain upright. Frank rammed his shoulder hard into Dexter's bent body, causing him to tumble against Ada with a crash, taking them both to the floor.

In a haze of black smoke and the smell of burning oil, Frank stared down at the two bodies. Ada's eyes had rolled back, her mouth was open and she was making gurgling sounds as blood flowed freely from the hole in her neck. Dexter, now on his back, his eyes staring into the distance, was as pale as a ghost with one hand to his stomach, half covering a serious wound where Ada had accidentally shot him when trying to kill Frank.

He lifted his revolver to take aim and finish what he had come to do.

But he didn't fire.

The job was done. He put his pistol back in his coat pocket, bent forwards and reached across to pull the carpetbag past Dexter's feet. It was unlatched, but the key remained in the brass lock. He opened it to see rows of notes, neatly placed in the half-filled the bag, along with a riverboat ticket to New Orleans. He added the money from the floor, clicked the latch closed, rotated the lock and withdrew the small key, putting it into the same pocket as his revolver.

Feeling the heat upon his back, Frank glanced towards the door, the small table where the ruptured lamp lay in pieces was now totally ablaze along with the carpet immediately below. The flames ran up the wall to lick against a small portrait painting. On the frame was the name Senator Roger Stannard, and he was looking Frank right in the eye.

As Frank was about to lift the carpetbag from the floor, the door flew open. Framed through the smoke haze was the man Frank has seen on door duty. 'What's going on…?' is all he got out before becoming transfixed by the bodies of Dexter and Ada on the floor with her handgun lying close by.

The man was blocking Frank's escape. 'Ada shot Dexter by mistake. You need to call the fire brigade,' is all he said.

The look upon the doorman's face was one of total bewilderment, then he became aware of the flames just behind the open door, which had shielded him from the heat. He pulled the door back a little to see, and this caused him to take fright: he turned and ran, yelling at the top of his voice 'Fire, fire, fire!' before grabbing the mallet to beat the enormous oriental brass gong. The sound boomed like a cannon in the open space of the marbled foyer.

Frank clutched the carpetbag, wrapped his arm around his face to protect himself from the heat, and made a dash for the door. In his rushed exit the bag struck the side of the doorframe, throwing him off balance and causing him to fall headlong on the tiled floor of the entrance hall, where he slid for several feet towards the base of the staircase. As he pushed himself to his feet, he looked up to see the mezzanine now congested with men scrambling to put on coats and shoes so that they might make their escape into the street with some dignity intact.

Flames and smoke from the office now billowed from the top of the door towards the underside of the mezzanine. The sight of this spectacle caused those coming down the staircase to panic, like a herd of stampeding cattle, animal instinct over-riding all composure in their effort to escape and survive. It was every man and woman for themselves, and those in the midst of this stampede were at risk of being injured.

Frank yelled at the top of his voice: 'Lily! Lily!' But as the noise of the gong continued, along with the mayhem on the staircase, it was impossible for his voice to carry. He squeezed on to the stairs, close to the banister, and began to climb against the crowd. Progress was slow and awkward, especially with the carpetbag, which was being knocked and almost ripped from his hand by those descending, so he raised it up to his chest, just as a young woman was shoved forcibly against him, jamming her face against the bag. 'Lily,' he said. 'Do you know where Lily is?'

The young woman was frantic to get away. 'Don't know,' she said. 'I haven't seen her. Got to get out.'

'I have to find Lily,' he said as the woman pushed past him, to be propelled by the crowd towards the front door.

Frank could feel the heat scorching the side of his face as the flames began to consume the fabric hanging from the walls. He hung on and turned his face away, and waited until the last of the throng hurtled down the stairs to join those fighting to get through the front door.

The smoke and the heat were now intense, making it difficult to breathe and see, and all the while Frank knew that time was running out. He dropped the carpetbag, put his arm across his face, and began to climb as fast as he could as visibility reduced with each step.

On reaching the mezzanine floor he called again: 'Lily! Lily!'

There was no reply.

He crossed to the far wall, his eyes stinging from the smoke, and felt his way along, searching for a door. A door handle hit his hip. He peered through the smoke and could just read 'Suite B'. He had to go one door back. He felt his way along the wall, his eyes now watering profusely and his breathing tight and short. His groping hand found the doorframe and the plate naming Suite C. He twisted the handle, pushed the door open and entered – it was pitch black. 'Lily, Lily!' he yelled. He went further, past the curtain, feeling about, grasping cushions and knocking a table to the floor, sending glasses crashing.

She wasn't there.

Frank made one more frantic search, calling both Lily's and Stanley's names in a desperate effort to find them. He got no response, and was now at risk of being unable to save himself: he had to go, and he had to go now.

When he made it back to the suite door he was met by heavy black smoke. He dropped to the floor in an effort to see and breathe, and crawled in what he hoped was the direction of the stairs. It was with relief that he found the balustrade and was able to pull himself along for some twenty paces, until suddenly he was falling down the stairs, tumbling and rolling like a log all the way to the bottom.

Frank crawled towards where he thought the entrance door was, his eyes now blind from excessive watering. So close, he thought, but not close enough – and then a hand grasped his shoulder and pulled him upright, pushing him into a second set of hands, then a third, a fourth and fifth: the firefighters had arrived and were bundling him out of the building.

TWENTY

A BLIND EYE

The Carpetbag

When Frank arrived on the street, he immediately felt
the cool air upon his face, and oddly, could hear the
sound of applause a little way off.

'Are there any more in there?' It was the voice of the
fire chief, his face close to Frank's and showing concern.

Frank could now make out the brim and badge on
his cap. He coughed in an effort to clear the taste from
his mouth, before answering, 'No, I didn't see anyone
else.'

'No one?'

'No.'

'On either the upper or lower floor?'

'None.'

'No one was calling for help?'

'No,' said Frank.

'Then you must be the last.' The chief patted his shoulder. 'Well done. We heard that someone was going up the stairs when all others were coming down. You are to be commended.'

Frank didn't believe there was much to commend him for. He now just hoped that somehow Lily had got out. He was led across to the far side of Cedar Street to join the large crowd now watching the building burn. A tin cup of water was handed to him. He took a mouthful, then splashed some of the water into his eyes, only to look up and see a sea of admiring faces nodding and saying, 'Well done, well done.'

'Frank, you are a marvel,' came a familiar voice just off to his left.

He turned to see Stanley sporting a broad smile. Lily was standing by his side, her face puzzled.

'Thank God,' said Frank, 'I thought you two might still be in there.'

Before Lily could respond, Stanley said with a grin, 'No, not a chance of us staying in there. When we heard that gong and the shout "fire, fire, fire!", we left immediately, didn't we Lily? Didn't even finish our champagne.'

Lily remained silent, her questioning eyes fixed on Frank.

'You know each other?' Stanley asked.

'Yes,' said Frank, 'I know Liv, but we have only just met.'

'That's him,' said a young woman, gripping the sleeve of an older man, his coat a little askew. 'That's him.'

'Are you sure?' the older man questioned.

'Yes, he was the one.'

'I believe this is yours.' The man lifted and pushed the carpetbag towards Frank.

Frank was having trouble comprehending. 'How?' he said. 'I dropped it on the staircase so I could return to the mezzanine.'

'Well, I nearly fell over it when I was coming down the stairs in the smoke, so I picked it up and carried it out. Nobody knew who it belonged to, except for this young lady.'

It was the woman who had been forced against Frank on the staircase.

'Therefore, I presume it is yours.' The man's tone indicated that he wasn't totally convinced.

'It is. I have the key in my pocket.' Frank felt around a little before holding it up.

The bag was placed at his feet.

'Thank you,' said Frank, reaching down and gripping the handles tight.

'Anything important in there?' he was asked, the man still standing before him.

'Just papers,' said Frank, 'lots of papers.'

The man looked somewhat dismayed that he had only saved a bag of papers.

'But very important papers. In fact, my future,' added Frank.

The saviour of the carpetbag seemed relieved, and offered, 'For business purposes, no doubt.'

'No doubt about it,' responded Frank.

'Good, as a businessman, I'm pleased that they have been returned to their rightful owner.'

'Yes,' said Frank, 'so am I.'

'Damn shame about the club going up in smoke,' said Stanley, looking over at the black clouds going skywards as the firefighters continued to dowse the flames. 'Maybe we should go. The law is arriving. Could be some awkward questions to answer.'

Frank could now see with some clarity as the mounted officers made their way towards the crowd, some of whom had begun to scurry away.

'Why don't we take a carriage to my place?' suggested Stanley. 'After such an ordeal, a glass or two of champagne is in order.' Stanley raised his eyebrows seeking acceptance to his offer. 'Lily,' he said, 'care to join us?'

She thought for a moment. 'No, I should stay with the girls.'

Frank leant over to her and said quietly, 'There's nothing here for you now. Not any more. The club has gone, and so has that way of life. It's time for you to leave.'

'To go where?' she asked.

'I'll get a carriage,' said Stanley, adding 'and then you can tell me about that carpetbag,' as he disappeared into the crowd.

Frank hadn't taken his eyes off Lily. 'Back to your family,' he said.

Lily pressed her lips tight. 'I want to, but…'

'Are you worried about not meeting your commitment to pay off the family farm?'

She shook her head.

'Then what is stopping you?'

Lily was reluctant to say, and began to fidget with a tightly twisted handkerchief wrapped around her fingers. 'It's…'

Frank waited, the colour of the reflected flames flicking warm upon her face.

'It's…?' he asked.

'It's Dexter and Ada. They won't let me go, even if the club has gone. I signed an agreement, and they will want me and all the girls to earn the money needed to rebuild the club.'

'You signed a contract?'

'Yes, all the girls had to.'

'Where are those contracts kept?

'Ada keeps them in the office. In the safe.'

'That's now gone,' said Frank, 'it's just ashes.'

'Dexter and Ada will still hold me to my word and they'll not let me go. They can be very forceful.'

'Dexter and Ada have gone too,' said Frank.

'Gone where?' asked Lily.

'The fire started in the office and they were the first to perish.'

Lily raised her hands and pressed her fingers to her lips. 'I thought everyone had been saved. All the girls have been accounted for. How? How could such a thing happen?'

'The fire was started from a pistol shot, fired by Ada, which shattered an oil lamp.'

'An accident?'

Frank paused before saying, 'Yes, she accidently shot the lamp. She didn't mean to do that.'

'I told Stanley that I had heard shots,' said Lily excitedly. 'He said it was just someone banging on the gong and that they were bound to get into trouble. Then we heard the shout of "Fire, fire, fire!".'

Frank leant in a little closer. 'No one has any hold over you any more, Lily.'

'If it is true, there is no reason for me to stay, is there?' It was a question by Lily to herself.

'It is true,' said Frank.

Lily still looked a little undecided.

'Would you let me escort you back to your parents?' he asked. 'I need to see them. I still owe your father some money.'

'Do you really?'

'I do, and it would be remiss of me not to settle now that I have come into…' Frank paused, before adding, 'an inheritance.'

'Recently?' asked Liv.

'Very,' replied Frank.

She thought for a moment. 'I will have to explain my time in St Louis. There will be many questions from my mother. But if you could…'

Frank knew what Liv was alluding to. 'Support your explanations to some things and turn a blind eye to others?' he said.

'Yes,' said Lily with a soft smile, 'by turning a blind eye.'

'Then I'll be forever blind,' said Frank.

Lily leant over and kissed him on the cheek.

'Why don't we go now?' he suggested.

'Now?'

'Yes, there is a riverboat heading south tonight and I have a ticket.'

'But my clothes, my shoes and we'll need two tickets,' said Lily.

'Your clothes and shoes may not necessarily reflect the style and dress of a governess.'

Lily agreed with a nod of the head.

'And yes, we could purchase another ticket or...'

'Or?' questioned Lily.

'Or maybe you could bunk in with me?'

When Stanley returned, Frank and Lily had gone.

The carriage driver asked him where they could be.

Stanley replied, 'Not sure, but I think they may be leaving St Louis.'

'Leaving now, in only the clothes they are standing in? Will they be OK?'

'Oh, yes,' said Stanley.

'You seem sure?' questioned the carriage driver.

Stanley caught a fleeting glimpse of a couple, she close and gripping the man's arm, while he held tight to the handles of a bag as they passed through the crowd towards the levée. 'I'm sure they will be just fine. They have a carpetbag.'

'A carpetbag? That seems hardly enough,' questioned the carriage driver.

Stanley watched the couple disappear. 'That all depends on what you have in it.'